PLAYING AT
MURDER

Previously published Worldwide Mystery titles by
KAREN McCULLOUGH

A GIFT FOR MURDER
WIRED FOR MURDER

PLAYING AT MURDER

KAREN McCULLOUGH

W🌐RLDWIDE

TORONTO • NEW YORK • LONDON
AMSTERDAM • PARIS • SYDNEY • HAMBURG
STOCKHOLM • ATHENS • TOKYO • MILAN
MADRID • WARSAW • BUDAPEST • AUCKLAND

W**O**RLDWIDE™

ISBN-13: 978-1-335-90148-4

Playing at Murder

First published in 2022 by Karen McCullough.
This edition published in 2024.

Recycling programs
for this product may
not exist in your area.

Harlequin Enterprises ULC
22 Adelaide St. West, 41st Floor
Toronto, Ontario M5H 4E3, Canada
www.ReaderService.com

Printed in U.S.A.

CAST OF CHARACTERS

Market Center Personnel

Heather McNeil, assistant to the director of the Washington, D.C. Commerce & Market Show Center

Janelle Addison, the Commerce & Market Show Center's director and Heather's superior

Scott Brandon, former police officer, security officer for the Center

Craig Vincelli, head of security

Mark Templeton and Sam Boresi, maintenance

Dennis Michaelton, shipping manager

Exhibitors

Donneywell: Lorene Donneywell, president and founder; Jessie O'Conner, her assistant; Olivia and Angelina Donneywell, Lorene's nieces; Kevin Donneywell, Olivia's son

Carrie Classics: Sam Schmidt, president; Janice Langley, product development manager; Ross Langley, Janice's son

GlamourThings Inc.: Emilia Grinkoff, president; Josef Grinkoff, her brother

Margolis & Carter: Joshua Carter

Juvenile Retail News: Daryl Hilderman, managing editor; Felicia, editor

Hanley: Oliver Hanley, Jeff

Others

Detective Peter Gilmont, the police detective assigned to the murder investigation

ONE

ARMIES OF SUPER-HEROES stood guard to the left of me, while lions, tigers, and bears gathered on the right. They all watched with silent concern as I zigged around an arsenal of armaments fueled by hydrogen dioxide and various mixtures of oxygen, nitrogen, and carbon dioxide. I faced my goal, Dougal the Dragon, head-on and stalked toward him. In my arms I cradled the all-important emergency medical supplies for his injured representative at this gathering. Heaven help us all if he couldn't be saved.

Ding dong. That was a bit of wild fantasy, but I enjoyed letting my imagination loose on this mission. The touch of whimsy provided some diversion from the noise and chaos of setting up the Games and Playthings Exhibition at the Washington D.C. Commerce and Market Center.

G&P, which was due to start the next day, was one of the largest trade shows for toys and games in the industry, and it brought the usual supply of problems and conflicts inherent in large events.

I tried to avoid being on the show floor as much as possible on set-up days. The constant banging of hammers, clanging of metal on metal, buzzing of electric screwdrivers, squeaking of dolly and cartwheels, warning chirps of the forklifts, and people shouting always induced a head-ache if I had to spend much time there. Not to mention having to pick my way around the pallets, crates, and boxes stacked everywhere, and dodging those squeaking dollies and chirping forklifts.

I still ended up spending more time on the floor than I would've liked. Territorial disputes and arguments over arrangements broke out with sadly human regularity, and a large part of my job involved keeping the peace. Trying to, anyway.

This assignment was different. I let go of the fantasy illusion as I reached the Donneywell Enterprises booth.

"Heather McNeil," I said to the person behind the only table set up in the booth space. "Assistant to the director of the Market Center. I was told you needed a sewing kit to repair one of your displays." I set the box down on the table where a young woman with long brown hair scraped back from her face and tied in a messy braid at the back looked up from collating and stapling pages.

She stared at me with a blank expression, glanced down at my badge, but said nothing. Her expression went from vacant to wary.

"Can I speak to the person in charge of the booth?" I asked when the silence stretched out too long.

A voice spoke from the back. "That would be me."

A woman in her late forties or early fifties stepped out from behind a pyramid of boxes at least a foot taller than she was. My first, none-too-kind impression of her was "overcooked." Her blonde hair had the straw-like texture resulting from too much chemical treatment for too long a time, and the spray-tanned skin of her face had been lifted once too often already. Tight jeans and a fashionably shoul-der-slit top showed off a slim figure that seemed to vibrate with contained energy. Good bones under the tight skin and lively green eyes made her attractive.

"Lorene Donneywell," she said, holding out a hand. "I heard you say you were with the Market Center staff." She had a strong New York accent.

"I'm the assistant to the director," I repeated. "I handle a lot of trouble-shooting issues for her. I've brought the sewing supplies you requested."

"Great. How long do you think it will take you?"

"Take me? To do what?"

"Fix the tear in Dougal." She pointed to the eight-foot-tall display dragon I'd used to identify their booth. The creature, which must've been as long as it was tall, occupied nearly a third of their allotted double space. Along the side of his back, a slit gaped open and leaked stuffing. Bits of cotton fluff clung to the green, plush fabric.

I hesitated, taken aback. "You requested a sewing kit, not a seamstress. I'm afraid I don't know the first thing about sewing. Not even sure how the thread gets through the needle."

Lorene rolled her eyes. "Why did they send you, then?"

"Because you asked for sewing equipment in a hurry. We got it as quickly as we could. We assumed you had someone on your staff who knew how to use it."

The woman's penciled-in eyebrows rose. "We all know what happens when you *assume* things."

I kept my smile in place, despite the irritation roiling inside. I had so much experience keeping my emotions under control, I could maintain a pleasant façade with barely a thought. "*Misunderstandings* happen when people aren't specific about what they need. Give me a minute and I'll see if I can find someone to come and make the repairs." I pulled out my phone but before I could press the button to turn it on, the girl I'd first met piped up.

"I can do it."

We both turned toward her, but Lorene spoke first. "Why didn't you say something sooner?"

The girl frowned at both of us. "No one asked."

I turned to hide my grin since Lorene didn't seem to appreciate the irony.

The woman rolled her eyes. "Get going, then. The show opens tomorrow, and I want it fixed as soon as possible."

I looked at her, then back at the younger woman. The latter's name tag said she was Jessie O'Conner. She appeared to be a couple of years younger than my own age of twenty-six.

"Would you check what we've got here and let me know if you need anything else?" I requested.

Jessie nodded and dug into the box, pulling out a thimble, a pair of scissors, and a package of needles. She rooted through several spools of thread and settled on one close to the color of the dragon's green fur. "It looks like everything I need." She turned to Lorene. "Should I do this before I finish collating the sell sheets?"

Undercurrents ran through the words. Challenge and traces of hostility for sure. Dislike perhaps. I wondered how long Jessie had worked for Lorene. She might be a temp hired for the show, though that wasn't the norm, especially for small operations where any contact with a potential buyer was too important to leave to someone outside the company. Maybe she'd only been hired for the day.

Lorene's expression showed only impatience as she waved an arm. "Yes. Yes. Fix Dougal. Then get back to the sell sheets. This all has to be ready to go tomorrow morning."

Jessie snipped a length of thread and put it through the

eye of the needle, managing that miracle in one try. Astonishing.

"What happened to it?" I glanced at the long split on the dragon.

"Beats me." Jessie went over to the stuffed creature, jammed cotton fluff back into it, and pushed the needle in at one end. "Maybe it happened at the factory, when they packed it." She grimaced. "Probably whoever took it out of the shipping carton wasn't careful with the knife." Her tone held no curiosity or concern.

Wouldn't that have been either her or Lorene? And it looked like a ripped seam rather than a random knife cut. But not my problem. "My number's here if you have any more issues." I left my card on the table. "Good luck. Let me know if you need anything else."

Jessie looked up and nodded before turning to glance back. Lorene had already disappeared behind the stack of boxes again, so she didn't see the glare the younger woman directed toward her.

"You're welcome, by the way," I said quietly as I walked down the aisle.

While I was delivering the dragon repair kit, Janelle, the director of the D.C Commerce and Market Center and my boss, had texted two more requests that needed to be checked out on the show floor. I headed toward the twelve hundred aisle instead of going back upstairs.

The phone buzzed again as I was settling a boundary dispute between booths. I excused myself to take the call and walked a few feet down the aisle.

"Heather?" Janelle sounded distracted. Setting up for a major show brought a lot of complaints, problems, and loose ends. The Games and Playthings show wasn't the biggest on our schedule, but it was large enough. Opportunities for shipments to get lost, boxes of products to stray, breakage, and other minor disasters abounded.

"What's up?" I asked.

"We've got a situation. Can't tell how serious yet. Craig and Scott are both on the way, but I need you at twenty sixteen."

My stomach lurched. At two previous shows words like those had presaged awful things happening. Things as bad as murder. Two months ago, at the Business Tech Expo, I'd witnessed a serious argument, later overheard one of the participants' murder, and then found the body. I still hadn't fully recovered from that trauma and the result of it, when a murderer had almost cornered me in the upstairs offices and attempted to make sure I couldn't share what I'd figured out.

"What is it?"

"Something about a weapon on the show floor. Someone reported seeing a gun."

TWO

MY STOMACH TWISTED and heart pounded even as I told myself it was probably nothing. "I'll bet there are hundreds of toy guns laying around. I almost tripped over a crate of them earlier. Some of them look real enough to fool people."

"I hope it's a toy," Janelle said. "But the person who called it in didn't think so. We can't take any chances. These days you can't be too careful. We have to check it out."

I agreed and ended the call.

I wrapped up the boundary settlement in a hurry by showing exactly where the lines were and asking a distributor of craft kits to move his boxes a few inches to the left to keep them on his side. Then I took off for the two thousand aisle. As I turned the corner there, I almost bumped into Craig Vincelli, head of security for the Market Center, and his assistant, Scott Brandon. The two contrasted starkly in appearance.

Craig was a big man in his mid-fifties, dark-haired and dark-eyed, solid in more ways than one. He wasn't always as well organized as we might hope, but in general he stayed on top of the Center's security needs. Despite his open, affable expression, you didn't want to mess with him. Craig had been a deputy sheriff in Maryland but quit when his doctor told him he needed a less stressful job.

By contrast, Scott Brandon was a little taller than Craig, a lot leaner, twenty-some years younger, blond with oddly light gray-green eyes. He was both sharper and harder than his boss. Scott was a former D.C. cop who refused to say why he was no longer with them. He kept his secrets close, even from me, and we've been dating for the last five months. But I'd also discovered his usual tensely stern expression was as deceptive as Craig's affability.

Despite the differences in appearance and attitude, they worked well together.

"Hey, what's happening?" I asked as I recovered my balance. "Janelle said something about a gun?"

"That's as much as we know," Scott answered as we headed for the booth.

"Probably a toy," Craig added. "They make ones that look amazingly realistic these days."

Scott grimaced. "It's a real problem for cops on the street."

"I imagine so."

We got to the Margolis and Carter booth, which took up three spaces, and identified ourselves as center staff to the man who seemed to be in charge. He introduced himself as Joshua Carter. Around the area four or five younger people pulled shrink-wrapped boxes of model cars, trucks, farm equipment, and even a couple of spaceships out of cartons and stacked them in towers that stuck up four to five feet from the floor. Several bins of stuffed animals and dolls were farther back. "Over here." The man led us toward one of the bins.

It lay in plain sight there, in a depression among the fuzzy bears, bunnies, dogs, and cats. About six inches long, matte black, and lethal looking, the pistol's ominous darkness was relieved only by what looked like an orange plug at the opening of the barrel.

Craig let out a harsh breath. "Airsoft," he said. "A toy."

Scott leaned over for a closer look, his face pulled into a frown. "Not exactly." He straightened but didn't reach down or touch it. "Look at the markings."

Craig checked again and swore.

I looked closer, too, and still had no idea what was bothering them. Some odd markings were engraved onto the side, including the word "Austria," which made no sense to me. "What is it?" I asked.

"It's not an Airsoft pistol," Scott answered. "It may be the real thing, or it might be a really good model of a Glock 17. In either case... Heather, could you get pictures of it? From different angles, then up close, with as much detail as you can."

"Okay." While I took pictures from above and the sides, he pulled a pair of latex gloves from a pouch on his belt and snapped them on.

He looked at the other people in the booth. "Does anyone have a bag I can use? Paper would be preferable but plastic will do."

Someone found a plastic grocery bag, which Scott took before he used a gloved hand to pick up the gun. "It's heavy." He did something to make the slide come off and looked down the barrel from the back. "Chamber's empty." Another flick and a piece slid down out of the handle. "Nothing in the magazine either. But definitely not a toy. Despite that." He pointed to the orange plug on the end.

Craig wrote in a notebook after looking around the booth. He checked his watch as well, so I assumed he was noting the details of when and where the gun had been found.

"What's up with this? That thing's a real gun?" Joshua Carter asked. "Where'd it come from?"

Craig stared at him. "You don't know? You've never seen this before?"

"Good God, no." His eyes widened and he leaned back from it. "I don't own a gun. Never have. Never will. Scared to death of the things. We don't make or distribute toy guns."

"You didn't see anyone drop it or leave it there?"

"No way. I'd've said something if I did."

We both scanned the booth, noting the people watching us with open interest. The story would make its way around the show quickly. "Anyone else see anything or know anything about it?" Craig asked.

Every one of them either said no or shook their heads. I didn't see any shifty looks or odd fidgets to make me think they were lying.

"Who found it?" Craig scanned the group.

A young woman slowly raised her hand. "I did. I noticed the Reiger dolls and the ComfortHouse animals were mixed together in the bin, which they shouldn't be, so I started sorting them out. I saw that under the animals."

"You didn't touch it?" Scott asked.

"I might've nudged it when I was moving things, but I didn't pick it up."

Scott and Craig each asked more questions, but all we learned was no one had seen anyone put the weapon there, no one could remember seeing anyone near the bins after they'd emptied bags of toys into them a few hours before, and no one had any idea who the gun might belong to. All denied ownership of it, though one of the young men said he had several pistols at home that he used for target practice. "Not a Glock, though. They're too expensive."

We took the bagged gun and left.

"What are you going to do with it?" I asked.

Scott and Craig looked at each other. "I think just lock it up upstairs for now," Scott answered.

"You're not going to give it to the police?" Scott had an uneasy relationship with his former employer, the Metro DC Police Department, and I wondered if that influenced his decision. "Don't want to deal with your former employers?"

I was poking the bear, but Scott's reticence frustrated me.

He didn't rise to the bait. Scott looked at Craig, who was in charge of security. Craig shrugged. "If we give it to MPD right now they'll toss it in their pile of weapons to be destroyed. I'd like to hold onto it and see if we learn anything more about it before I do that."

"I guess it makes sense."

"There are several peculiar things about this," Scott added. "The orange tip on a real, live-ammo Glock, for one."

"The orange plug thing is supposed to signal it isn't a real gun." That was from one of our rules—any unpackaged firearms brought in had to be marked as either disabled or a toy with a brightly colored marker. It came up occasionally at the toy show and at a science fiction convention held here later in the year.

Scott glanced into the bag again. "Depends on how you define 'real gun.' BB-guns and Airsoft pistols can fire pellets at speeds high enough to do significant damage, but they don't use bullets with gunpowder, so they don't have the same deadly force. But the orange plug isn't completely a lie either, since it's not loaded."

"Okay. What else is odd about it?"

"A Glock is an expensive gun. Not the kind of thing you abandon lightly."

A horrible thought occurred to me. "Unless it's already

been used in a crime. Maybe someone needed to dispose of one. Does it have a serial number that could be traced?"

"Yes and no. It has a serial number, but there's no easy way to trace it."

"Isn't there a database to look it up?"

"Not exactly. There's actually a law against the government having a computerized gun registry."

I was shocked. "You're kidding. That's crazy."

Scott's mouth twisted in a wry frown. "Tell me about it. There is a national center, and the staff there is amazingly good at tracing weapons used in crimes. They do it with paper records. But they're overwhelmed. No point in submitting a weapon we don't know anything about."

"I guess hanging onto it for now makes the most sense. The whole thing makes me uneasy, though, and I'm not sure why."

"Maybe that was the point," Scott said. "To make people uncomfortable."

"But why?"

He hesitated and took my hand for a moment. "I don't have any more answers than you do." Then he smiled, which erased some of the hard lines of his face and made my heart stutter. "There's probably some ridiculously absurd, but innocent reason for why it was there. Let's don't manufacture trouble."

My phone buzzed and he released my hand. "That's probably the trouble bell ringing now." I pulled it out of its case on my belt.

His grin broadened, showing off the deep grooves on either side of his mouth, reminding me just how attractive he could be. Hormones wanted to come out and play. He gave me a quick hug. "I'm taking this upstairs. Good luck with the next crisis."

THREE

Tuesday

I NODDED AS I lifted the phone to answer Janelle's call. I had to tamp down a strong urge to throw myself at Scott and beg him to kiss me right there. Yup, that would look professional.

"Another disagreement," Janelle said, sighing into the phone. "Something about a magazine article, as best I could tell. Called in by people at a neighboring booth. Four thirty."

I let out a short breath as I ended the call. That aisle was clear on the other side of the exhibit floor, and even though I wore comfortable shoes, my feet were beginning to hurt. It was after four, and I'd been standing or walking almost the entire day.

Still, I hoofed it to the other end of the large hall. At least it was quieting down now as exhibitors put the final touches on their booths in preparation for the opening of the show tomorrow. Some had already finished and left. Sales meetings and rallies would enliven restaurants and hotels around the area this evening. Thank heaven, I didn't have to be involved in any of those.

In the increasingly quiet space, I heard the raised voices before I even reached the aisle and turned toward the back.

"…someone should know better than this. You don't

disrespect one of your best customers this way. We'll have to consider pulling—"

The diatribe cut off abruptly as the three people standing on the edge of the magazine's booth heard me coming and looked up. Others lingered nearby, but all were quiet, watching the contretemps.

I walked up to the group of two men and one woman and introduced myself, including my title, and waited for them to return the courtesy. The red-faced young man standing on the booth's carpet, leaning on a small podium, looked relieved. He held out a not-quite-steady hand and said, "Daryl Hilderman, managing editor of *Juvenile Retail News.*"

I looked at the others. The woman extended her hand and said, "Janice Langley, Carrie Classics Product Development Manager." I shook it. The woman was a squeezer with a strong grip, but fortunately she kept it brief. She glanced at her companion. "Sam Schmidt, president of Carrie Classics."

Schmidt gave me a sharp, brief nod and reluctantly took my hand as well.

"Now, what seems to be the issue?" I asked. "You're creating a disturbance on the floor."

Schmidt launched back in with vigor and vinegar. "The issue is this idiot's magazine ran a huge, blockbuster announcement of a major product release we're doing and then put a competitor's ad on the facing page instead of the one we paid for. Paid a huge amount for. We were promised that placement. It was essential. Now it looks like Vestin is a distributor of the World Traveler Dolls instead of us."

Hilderman took advantage of the other man's need to draw a breath. "And I've been trying to tell him I'm the managing editor. I have nothing, *nothing*, to do with ad placement. He needs to talk to his sales rep. I wasn't responsible, and I can't do anything about it."

The woman, Janice Langley, watched the interchange with an odd glitter in her eyes. Anger, but something more and I couldn't guess what the rest was. As Schmidt started to speak again, she put a hand on his arm. He stopped before the first word came out.

"We're very frustrated," Langley said. "It was so disappointing. Especially after— But that's not relevant here. I think Sam just needed to blow off some steam."

"Understandable. Who is your sales rep for the magazine?"

"Avery Masters." Janice said it quietly, but the words dripped poison nevertheless.

"I'll be happy to leave a message for him," Hilderman offered. "I don't know what he can do, but I'm sure he'll try to make it right somehow."

"Not much he can do now," Schmidt said. "Other than refund what we paid for the ad. But we really wanted that placement." Veins stood out on his neck. The combination of that with the man's bulk, the tension displayed by his fisted hands, and his very red face made me worry about him having a stroke or heart attack.

"We did," Janice Langley agreed. "But I guess there's nothing we can do about it now." Her anger was better contained than Schmidt's, but possibly more dangerous for it.

"I understand your frustration," I told them. And I did. The kind of opportunity offered by the article didn't happen often. "But there's nothing more you can do right here and right now. Tomorrow you can talk to your sales rep, but for now I'd suggest going somewhere to have a good dinner and a drink. If you need some suggestions, there are several good places nearby. I even have free drink coupons for the Fabulo Lounge, right down the street." I pulled the coupons out of a pocket and handed two to each of the three people. This was a new thing for us. I didn't love being a shill for a bar, but I'd already found those coupons could help mollify irritated clients.

Schmidt and Langley both accepted them with minimal enthusiasm, but they did take them.

"There's nothing you can do now," I repeated. "I'm sure someone will get in touch with you about the ad." I looked to Daryl for confirmation. He nodded. The other two still looked aggrieved but accepted the inevitable and turned away. A few steps down the aisle, Schmidt stopped and whirled around. "We'll expect to hear from Avery Masters very soon. Or better yet, Mark Ellisboro." With that, he stomped off.

The editor, Daryl, gave a huge sigh of relief as they disappeared. "Thank you. I do feel bad for them. It was a big, big gaffe by someone. Heads may roll. Thank God it wasn't me, though, and there's nothing much I can do for them."

"Except let them vent."

He looked uneasy. "Yeah. But for a while I thought they might do more than vent. Schmidt looked ready to choke me. Or have a stroke. Not sure which would be worse. And that woman, Janice Langley… It was strange. It seemed like she was trying to calm him, but it really only made his anger worse. Don't know what's going on there."

"Who is Ellisboro?"

"Our publisher. The big boss. I think he's the one who courted the account, so he'll probably need to do the damage control. Don't envy him that."

"I don't either. If you're okay, I need to go," I said.

"Yes, thank you. I'm glad you showed up before something bad could happen. I owe you."

"I'll keep it in mind."

He turned and began gathering papers as I walked away.

The show floor had gotten quiet, and I checked the time. Five fifteen. Nearly everyone had left. I texted Scott to tell him I was ready to go.

Most normal days he drove me home, and we'd stop to get dinner along the way. Not that we had many normal days. It was one of the things I loved about the job. There were always new things going on and new challenges. Not all of them were good or positive, but I like that a big part of my job involved finding ways to make people happy. Or happier anyway, since I couldn't always satisfy everyone.

I asked Scott about the gun over dinner at one of our favorite places for weeknights. On weekends, the steakhouse was too crowded and noisy, but on a Tuesday, it held just a few families. The quiet corner spot we favored was almost always open.

He took a big bite of his burger, chewed, and swallowed before answering. "I've put it away in a locked cabinet for now. Until someone claims it, or we have reason to worry about it, there's not much else to do."

"But who would've left it there? And why? Especially if it's an expensive gun, it doesn't seem like something someone would put down and forget."

Scott took a drink of his soda and set it down. "It puzzles me, too. If we found it almost anywhere else, I'd assume someone was disposing of a weapon used in a crime. But that seems kind of absurd here. The show isn't open to the public, and only exhibitors were there today."

He stopped to take another bite. "I can't think of many good reasons why it would be there. An accident is possible, but not likely. So why else? Send a message to someone?"

"A threat, you mean?"

"Probably, but there are other possibilities. The gun wasn't loaded."

"And it had the orange plug in it. I don't get that either."

"The orange plug might just have been a way to get it onto the show floor," Scott said.

"Maybe we should ask a few questions at the booth to-morrow."

Scott gave me a stern look. He didn't approve of my efforts at solving crimes in the past, and I'd scared him half to death at the end of the Business Tech show when a killer had nearly strangled me. But he got points for refraining from telling me to back off. "I'll stop by and ask questions. With it being the first day of a big show, I'm betting you'll have your hands full." *Heading me off?* Yes, he'd do that.

"I suppose you're right."

He reached across the table to take my hand in his. "If I learn anything interesting, you'll know about it."

I believed him. There were things Scott hadn't shared with me. I didn't totally understand why, and sometimes it frustrated me, but if he made a promise, he'd keep it.

Changing the subject, he said, "I saw a booth with amazing chemistry sets this morning. I wasn't really interested in science as a kid, but who can resist a chemistry set?" His eyes lit with enthusiasm. "I had one when I was ten or twelve. Really basic, but I had fun fooling around with it. My mother worried I'd blow up the house, but the worst thing that happened was I made this inky liquid which spilled on the countertop and left weird stains. Took a lot of scrubbing to get rid of them. And I ruined a few towels in the process."

"Did your mom make you get rid of it?"

"Nah. I did pay for new towels from my allowance. I lost interest in it after that. Too much work."

LATER, AFTER I was home and in bed, trying to fall asleep, I kept thinking about the gun. The image crept into my dreams and brought memories of two other murder victims whose bodies I'd found. Neither of them had been shot, but they'd been dead, violently dead, and I'd never forget either as long as I lived.

I woke up early the next morning, though that was more habit than anything else. Particularly on opening day for a show, I liked to give myself plenty of time for a stop at the coffee shop on the way to the Metro station, and then time in the office to get some things sorted out before the circus revved up.

The coffee and my inbox were both half-empty by the time Janelle arrived twenty minutes after I did. She waved at me as she passed by going to her office. I usually gave her fifteen minutes or so to get settled before I went in to discuss anything about the day we needed to cover.

I didn't have to wait long. She came out again after five minutes, holding her cell phone and looking concerned.

"You handled something for a Lorene Donneywell yesterday, didn't you? The name is familiar, but I can't place it."

It took me a moment, too. "Dougal the Dragon. Yes, I took them a sewing kit to repair a torn stuffed dragon. Why? Is she complaining again?"

Janelle drew a breath and let it out on a long exhale. "Not likely. She was killed by a hit-and-run driver last night, going from a restaurant to her hotel."

FOUR

"DANG." I FELT as though I'd been punched in the gut. At least this time, I didn't hear the murder and didn't find the body.

Wait. It was probably just an accident. Why was I even thinking otherwise? Hit-and-run accidents happened all too often in D.C.

"Where was she staying?" I asked.

"The ManorBright Hotel up the street."

So, it had happened nearby.

"What are the police saying about it? An accident or deliberate?"

Janelle gave me an odd look. "We've had too many murders around here in the last few months. You're starting to see them everywhere. As far as I know, this was an unfortunate accident."

I let out a long breath. "Of course."

"I got a call from Pete Gilmont letting me know. It was just a courtesy call, though, since they knew she was here for the show." I didn't miss her expression when she mentioned the D.C. detective who'd investigated previous cases here. She'd never admitted it, but I think she had something going with him. The change was fleeting, though, turning into a tight frown. "What happened with her yesterday?"

Janelle's expression remained fixed while I related my encounter with the Donneywell woman. "Sounds like she wasn't a pleasant person."

"Well, yeah."

"And therefore a candidate for murder?"

"Point taken. I'm seeing crimes where there probably aren't any. Do we know what's going to happen with their booth? There was only that one other girl there yesterday, and she didn't seem like the take-charge type."

Janelle's frown changed into a grin. Kind of an evil grin. It reminded me that even in her mid to late forties, she was still an attractive woman. The lines around her eyes and lips showed good humor. "Better check in with her then."

I would, but I didn't have to be happy about it.

"Hey," she said. "I've got some good news, too. Dennis Michaelton is coming back to work tomorrow."

"Wow, really?" The shipping manager had been out on leave for almost six months now for cancer treatment.

Janelle nodded. "The doctors say he's in remission. He says he's feeling pretty well recovered from the chemo and ready to get back to work."

"The maintenance people will be glad to hear it." They'd been having to do most of the work to cover for Dennis's absence.

"No doubt. They're putting up a 'Welcome Back' banner in the shipping area later today." She turned toward her office and signaled for me to follow. "I've got a couple of other things for you to check out as well." I took the sticky notes she picked up from her desk and held out. She pointed to a note on a lime green slip of paper. "This is an odd one. You'll probably need to check with Andrea on it. People claiming they're in the wrong spot."

Andrea was the show manager for this event. Something

more must be at play here since normally Janelle would've given the note directly to her to deal with. For some reason my boss wanted my take on the dispute or thought it was something I should handle directly.

A visit to the Donneywell Enterprises booth would be my first stop, however, after I finished the coffee and took care of some paperwork sitting on my desk. I didn't want to go down and talk to the girl, Jessie was it? Or whoever might be in the booth now. If anyone was.

But duty called and I answered. The doors to the show floor opened at nine. I arrived a few minutes later and entered amid the throng of excited attendees. Everyone started the first day of the show with incredible enthusiasm and vigor. By late this afternoon, they'd be dragging and grumpy, tired and overloaded with information and product brochures.

Jessie sat at the table in the front of the booth, looking as glum as she had the previous day. Recognition flashed in her eyes as I approached, but that was the only response. On the show floor, I rarely took anyone's reaction to me personally.

"Hi. I heard about Lorene. I'm so sorry. What a terrible thing."

The girl just shrugged.

"It's pretty shocking," I said.

Jessie didn't seem grief-stricken. In fact, I couldn't detect much emotion at all. "Shocking, yeah. Didn't expect it." If anything, she sounded bemused and puzzled.

"You worked for her?" I asked.

"Yeah."

"You were her assistant?"

"Yeah. Sort of."

"Sort of?"

Jessie looked around the booth. "I did what she told me to do. She paid me for it. Not well, but she did pay."

"The company is based in New York? You live there?"

"Actually, we have a crappy little office in Newark. Lorene keeps—kept—a post box at a place in Manhattan. Made us look classier, she said."

"Oh. What happens now?" I felt like an attorney cross-examining a hostile witness.

"Don't know exactly. Her nieces are on the way. Guess they'll take care of things."

"Do they work in the business, too?"

"One of them does. Kind of."

I struggled to hold onto patience. "What does 'kind of' mean?"

"When she feels like it." Finally, her calm broke. "The princess occasionally deigns to come into the office and putter around." A bitter laugh interrupted her words. "I suppose she'll actually have to do some real work now that Lorene's gone. Or maybe she'll dump the whole thing." Some of the ugly sarcasm drained from her expression, leaving it looking more gloomy than angry. "That's a crock, isn't it? Lorene worked so hard to build this business. Struggled, lied, cheated, seduced, and deceived her way to success. For what? She dies before she even gets to see it pay off." Another exaggerated shrug. "I guess I'll be out of a job soon."

"What do you mean?"

"If the niece sells the company, the new owners probably won't need me. Even if I do know more about the business than anyone else."

"You don't think the niece will want to keep running it herself?"

"Doubt it. She was only interested in the money." A hint of malice underlay Jessie's words.

"That wasn't what I was asking about, though. I meant the part about Lorene cheating and lying to build up the company."

Jessie squirmed in her seat. "Shouldn't have said that. I don't really *know* anything."

I kept quiet. A lot of people would rush to fill the empty space, but Jessie wasn't one of them. I doubted a direct approach would get anything out of her either, so I went indirect. "You think you'll have trouble getting another job?"

She stared straight ahead. "I don't know. It's not like this one was so great."

"I got the idea Lorene could be difficult to work with."

"Understatement. She was a bi— Anyway, yeah. Difficult. Don't expect the niece to be much better."

"Can you take care of the booth for the show? Write orders and things like that."

"Sure, if the princess will pay me to do it."

"The princess? Lorene's niece? Is she coming here to the show?"

"Got a text this morning saying she'll be here later today."

"We'll need to get a badge for her. What's her name?"

"Livvy Donneywell. Olivia."

"Does she know enough about the business to handle things here?"

"Good question. Probably not. But they're going to make a ton of money anyway."

I raised an eyebrow and Jessie gave me a strange, where-have-you-been-hiding look. She glanced at the huge green stuffed dragon at the corner of the booth, the one she'd repaired yesterday. "You haven't seen the trailers for the Dougal the Dragon movie? You don't have kids, do you?"

"No kids. Not married. Not much time for movies if they're not streaming."

"It looks pretty crappy, if you ask me. But it will come out a few weeks before Christmas and all the little kids are going to want a Dougal Dragon under the tree this year. Or at least the parents will think so."

"I see."

Jessie nodded. "Not sure how Lorene got the exclusive license for the Dougal toys, but I can take a guess."

Again I waited, but she wasn't ready to share any of those guesses. Professionalism meant I shouldn't be encouraging her to gossip about her employers. Even her deceased employer. Maybe especially her deceased employer. I fought a brief internal battle. My better half won.

"I'll make sure we have a badge ready for Olivia. And you have my card. Give me a call if there's anything you need."

"Okay."

I pulled out the sticky notes Janelle had given me and proceeded to the booth noted on the top slip. For the next hour I answered questions about what food and drinks could be served on the show floor, found a printer for an exhibitor whose order forms had been lost in shipping, suggested a restaurant for a dinner to woo a potential big client, and settled a dispute about loud music in a neighboring booth, by the simple expedient of asking them to turn it down.

The most interesting stop was at a booth which featured kits of interlocking electronic components that let children build circuits to make noises and light. They came in various levels of complexity. Some looked more complicated than I'd ever want to tackle, though the flying saucer launcher looked like fun. I wasn't any more a science nerd than Scott, but I still would've loved these kits when I was a kid.

"We're an authorized dealer for these," a man's voice said from the other side of a huge stack of boxes. "We have a full assortment product line in all price ranges."

"Excuse me," I said. "I'm Heather McNeill, I work for the Market Center. You said you had a problem."

"Oh, sorry." He came around the display to hold out a hand and introduce himself before he glanced away. "The problem is at the back. One of our racks is broken. I know it's our responsibility, but I wondered if you could help us locate a hardware store that might deliver a part."

I went with him and checked the rack. A broken brace let the shelves rock to the side.

"I think we can do better than that," I said. "Give me a moment." I called down to maintenance and explained the situation.

"Mark will be there in a couple of minutes," the supervisor said.

I had mixed emotions as I told the man in the booth one of our maintenance people should be able to fix it. Being around Mark was personally awkward. He'd had a crush on me for a long time and was sure I secretly returned the regard, so it didn't sit well with him when Scott came on board and we started dating.

Since I had other obligations, I took the coward's way out and excused myself, promising them someone would be there shortly.

With the lime green sticky note still to check on, I made my way over to the six hundred aisle.

The booth was one of the small ones, just one space. When I got a look at it, my jaw dropped. Pretty literally. I stared for a couple of minutes with my mouth drooping open. Then I shut it so hard my teeth smacked together before I approached.

FIVE

Wednesday

THE SINGLE-SPACE booth was completely contained in a large, rainbow-hued tent. Dangly edges of the top spilled over into the neighboring displays. Amazing we hadn't gotten any complaints about it. Or about other features of the booth setup, like the wispy streamers of glitter-crusted, cottony fabric hanging from the rim at one-foot intervals along the side I could see. Or the odd music drifting from within, something that sounded like a scratchy old recording of children singing nursery rhymes accompanied by a tinkly piano.

An enormous banner stretched across the width of the tent above the open front proclaimed it the home of "GlamourThings Inc., Acesories for Twelve Inch Fashion Dolls." Apparently, their marketing department didn't include a proofreader.

Banks of lights on poles illuminated the interior, highlighting racks of doll-sized clothing, shoes, jewelry, and handbags in blister packs on the left side, and a table featuring plastic dollhouses—or more accurately doll-sized mansions—and cars, shops, pools, and water fountains on the right.

That left about eight square feet of space for visitors. Guess they weren't expecting big crowds. At the time I approached, only two people were visible inside, a small woman and a much taller man who stood in the middle of the area. Before I got to the entrance, the tall man turned away, tucking a piece of paper in his briefcase, and bent his neck to exit the tent.

The woman watched me approach, spreading a welcoming grin across her face. I've noted before that with some people, you could actually see the effort it took to assume the salesman's smile.

Otherwise, she reminded me of the garden gnomes I've seen at gift and landscaping shows with her round, wrinkled, tan face, stubby nose, and wide eyes. A thick layer of makeup only emphasized the resemblance. Long, dangling silver earrings, a splashy, spangled red vest over a loose white shirt, long green broomstick skirt, and gray boots with two-inch heels completed her distinctive look.

"Emilia Grinkoff." She held out a hand and I shook it.

The pasted-on smile faded when I identified myself as Market Center staff. I followed her gaze when she looked out of the tent, scanning the aisle. No one else approached. She let her expression go from welcoming to angry in a flash.

"You're here to talk about my complaint? I certainly hope you can get this sorted out and get us moved to where we belong."

"Where do you belong?" I asked.

"On the one-thousand aisle. It's supposed to be a bigger space than this."

"I assume you checked with Andrea, the show manager, about your location."

The woman rolled her eyes. "She insists we signed up for a one-space booth. Well, we did. But I called a couple of weeks ago and asked to change it."

The deadline for booth applications had been four months ago and the floor plan had been finalized for at least two months. "A couple of *weeks* ago?"

"I think it was that. Anyway, the girl who answered took my details and said she'd see what she could do. I didn't hear anything more. So of course, I figured it was okay and done."

"You didn't check back to see if anything had been arranged?"

The woman shook her head, setting those dangly earrings swaying. "Didn't think it was necessary."

"But you never heard from us about it? Did you get an invoice for a larger space?"

"I don't know. My assistant handles things like that."

"Did you get a confirmation for a new booth assignment?"

"I think so."

"Do you have it with you?" I asked.

"What?"

"The booth confirmation. Or the receipt?"

She gave me a blank look. "No. Why would I?"

I was beginning to understand why Janelle had passed this one off to me. Andrea would've lost her mind several minutes ago. Even my patience was feeling stretched.

"Do you remember who you spoke with when you asked to change the booth?"

"No, not really."

I sighed but tried to keep it mostly invisible. "I'll check with the show manager about it, but at this point…" I looked around to help make my point. "The show is at capacity and there aren't any open spaces, so I don't know where we could move you."

She gave me a narrow-eyed, mouth-twisting grin. "I

know a couple of people you could move. Sharpleys is four aisles over. They have a bigger space, and they don't do nearly the business we do."

"That may be, but if they paid for the bigger space, we can't move them out of it. In any case, it's a bit late to be shuffling booths."

"I'm sure I could get some people to help." She glanced out at the aisle. "I don't think our neighbors are going to appreciate the crowds we draw."

"If their booths get some attention from people waiting to get in here, I doubt they'll mind. Anyway, we only move booths in extreme circumstances." *Like the one we had a couple of months ago when I found a dead man in one of the booths.* I shuddered and told myself I wouldn't go there. I needed to get away. "I'll talk to the show manager and see if she has any record of your request. Then we can go from there."

"So we just have to manage here? Is that what you're telling me?"

"For the moment, yes. I can't make any promises about what else we can do. But I will ask."

Her mouth crooked to one side; it wasn't a pleasant grin. "You do that, honey. I guess we'll have to make do here."

Why did the words sound more like a threat than a promise?

I added a reminder to my phone to check on her booth request when I went back upstairs, stopped by the registration booth to let them know we needed a badge for Olivia Donneywell, and headed down to the food court for lunch.

I debated between a hot dog and a burrito and went with the latter because I could convince myself it was a healthy choice. It had beans and lettuce on it, so it counted for my vegetable allotment.

Spotting Craig and Scott at a table in the corner, I headed over to join them. As I sat down, Craig wiped his mouth with his napkin, stood, and picked up his empty plate and cup. "Sorry to run, but I just finished, and I have an appointment in ten minutes. Scott can fill you in."

Scott nodded to me as he opened the box of salad in front of him and took a few bites. I managed to get around some of the burrito before I asked, "Fill me in on what?"

"The gun we found at the Margolis & Carter booth. I went back there this morning to talk to them some more—as best I could, around the customers pouring through. They're a popular company. I gather they mostly import cheap goods from Asian countries and sell at low prices. I wonder if someone resents that and was trying to send a message?"

"They're far from the only ones. I'll bet there are at least a dozen companies doing the same thing here."

Scott's mouth twitched in a frown as he chewed a mouthful of salad and swallowed. "I didn't learn much more. They have six people here at the show. We met Joshua Carter, the co-owner of the company, yesterday. His partner, Dave Margolis, didn't get here until this morning. The other four are all young, early- to mid-twenties at most. I think we probably saw all but one of them yesterday."

"Order-taker is an entry-level job. Not much salesmanship needed with products like those other than to convince a customer to order more of each item. I expect they have memorized scripts for the process."

"Probably. I talked to each of them for a couple of minutes. They all struck me as being exactly what they seemed. The young people are mostly in their first job, one they hope is starting them on a successful career. I got no sense of ulterior motives from any of them. No one saw anyone drop a gun in, but it had to happen after one of the girls filled up the bin with stuffed animals. That was around eleven."

He stopped for another bite of salad. "I checked the videos but there was so much traffic along the aisles my view of the bin was repeatedly blocked. I never saw anyone put anything into it, but it could easily have been hidden by passing dollies and carts loaded with boxes. There were several times when no one in the booth was looking in that direction."

I studied his face for a moment. "It's bothering you, isn't it?"

He set his fork down and took a drink before answering. "It's such an oddity. A real gun, an expensive gun, made to look harmless even though it isn't, dropped into a bin full of toys. Why would someone do that? I don't like things so out of place. It makes the hairs on the back of my neck twitch." He rubbed his cheek.

"We thought it might be a threat to someone."

"But who? No one there seems anything but puzzled by it. If it's a message, it doesn't seem to be reaching the intended recipient—whoever that might be."

I set down my burrito as a thought crossed my mind. "Maybe it has reached the intended target."

"Us?" His sandy brows rose as his eyes widened. "Why would anyone threaten us?"

"Or warn us? Telling us trouble is coming? Someone making a statement he or she can do whatever they want on the floor, bring in whatever weapons they want, right under our noses?"

"We've already had plenty of trouble on the exhibition floor in past shows." He said it carefully and I wasn't sure whether he was implying I was looking for problems where there weren't any or if he was speculating there might be a possibility for more issues.

"Not sure where you're going with that."

His mouth twisted into a crooked grin. "Neither am I. Just trying to make some sense of it. It's also possible someone planted it for use later, hoping it would stay hidden until needed. And even if someone saw it, the plug to make it look like a toy would help disguise it. The girl who found it said she didn't see it until she'd moved a couple of things, so it wasn't in plain sight all the time."

I swallowed a bite of burrito that stuck in my throat for a moment. "An ominous thought. But whoever put it there had already gotten it onto the show floor. Why hide it in such an obvious place? It was too easy to find in the bin. There must be plenty of other, less obvious places, if he or she had to stow it somewhere."

"Maybe. If it was someone in a small booth there might not be any place to hide it. But what would be the point?"

"Someone planning to shoot up the place?"

The smile reached his eyes this time, lighting them up. He shook his head. "How likely do you think that is?"

I shut my eyes against the memories. "I didn't think murder would be likely either. But it's happened. Twice."

The smile disappeared. "Heather, are you—?"

I cut him off. "I'm fine. I'm functioning. I can't get rid of all the memories, but they're not making me crazy. Really."

He set down his fork, reached over, and put his hand on top of mine. "Good. So stop worrying so much. That's my job. Let me handle it. You've got plenty on your plate already."

I suspect he knew how good the contact felt to me. How reassuring and promising. I wanted more but needed to remain professional. For now. "True. And there's not a lot more we can do about it right now."

My phone buzzed. I sighed as I pulled my hand loose from his to look at it. "Janelle," I said to Scott and answered it. "What's up?"

"Raised voices," she said. "At the registration booths. Sounds like two people claiming the same name tag."

"I'm on it."

I quickly downed the few remaining bites of burrito while Scott finished his salad. In a corner away from the crowd, he gave me a quick kiss, then left to check in with Craig, while I headed for conflict-resolution duty at the registration area. I'd much rather have stayed for more kissing.

SIX

Wednesday

TEN REGISTRATION BOOTHS stretched across a third of the lobby, but only two were manned at the time, and only one had customers present. Two women stood in front of that one, glaring at each other, while the clerk behind the desk tapped at her computer and tried to ignore them. Relief spread across her face when she looked up and saw me approach.

"Ladies, can I help you?" I asked, interrupting a low-pitched hissing exchange between the two.

Both turned to face me and spoke at once.

"They had a badge with my name on it, so obviously I was expected," the first one, a tall, well-curved, forty-ish woman with long, dark hair said.

"But I was here first, and they gave *me* the badge." The other woman was a few inches shorter, several years younger, much thinner, and her mousy brown hair had brilliant blue streaks. She frowned at me. "If you know about *her,* why wasn't I included?" She showed me the badge and I read Olivia Donneywell's name on it.

I held up a hand. "First, can I get your names? And why you're here?"

"Olivia Donneywell," the taller woman said. "Lorene

Donneywell was my aunt. I guess you know what happened to her. I'm supposed to take over the business in her absence."

"Angelina Donneywell." That was the one with the blue streaks. "Call me Angie. Lorene is my aunt, too. And I'm pretty sure she left the business to us jointly."

"You're sisters?" I asked.

"Cousins. Our fathers were Lorene's two brothers. We're the only kids any of them had."

"I'm sorry for your loss. Her death must've been a terrible shock to you. I'm glad you could both get here so quickly."

The women shot pointed glances at each other and shrugged. "It was a shock," Angelina said. "Aunt Lorene was…"

Olivia picked it up. "Alive. Very much alive."

"And now she's not," Angelina added. "It's like the space she occupied is empty now. Echoing. It's going to be hard to fill her shoes."

Olivia drew a sharp breath. "But that's my problem now."

"Not just yours. Both of ours."

"We need to find out exactly what her will says. She told me she was going to leave me in charge of the business. I was even training with her to take it over some day."

Angelina glowered at her. "Yeah, you showed up at her office every other month to soak her for cash."

Olivia's voice rose when she answered, "Like you never asked her for any favors, either. I heard about the thing in Hartford, you know."

Angelina's face went red. "And she never bailed that kid of yours out of a couple of scrapes? Come on."

Before either could say anything further, I stepped between them to get to the registration desk counter. "No more, please. This is not our business, but if you create any kind of disruption to the show it *will* be. We'll get badges for both of you. I'll need each of you to fill in this form and show me your IDs."

Mercifully they remained quiet while they completed the registration forms and produced their drivers' licenses. The woman behind the desk entered their information into the computer, got another badge printed up, and put it together for Angelina.

"Booths 818 and 820," I said, as I handed over the badges. "Remember. We don't tolerate any disruption on the exhibit floor."

That wasn't quite true, seeing as how we tolerated all sorts of weird stuff some people would consider disruptive, but they didn't need to know that.

"Oh. I expect my son will be joining me in the next day or so," Olivia added. "Can you make up a badge for him?"

I picked up another registration form from the desk. "Fill this out and bring it back, then call me when he gets here, and I'll approve it." I handed her my card.

I watched them walk away, making a mental note to check back with them later. I got the impression Jessie didn't like either of them. I don't think she expected both to descend on the booth. How would she deal with the two together? Not to mention, the son sounded like he could be trouble.

For the moment I had no particular assignment, so I went back to the show floor to do a walk-through. A surprising number of people poured out the doors and headed down the escalator as I went up. I glanced back. The crowd surged toward the conference rooms, so there must be a popular speaker or an important issue being discussed.

The noise level on the exhibit floor was noticeably lower,

though it was a long way from silent. I wandered down a couple of aisles, bemused by the variety of toys available. I was particularly intrigued by a display of ingenious puzzles and a set of craft kits I would've loved to have had when I was younger.

Or maybe even now. I might have to ask if they'd sell me one when the show was over. A lot of merchants sold or gave away display products at the end rather than pay to ship them back. Not that I had much free time for play, but I should maybe try to relax a bit more. I liked the idea of it.

I passed the booth for *Juvenile Retail News* magazine, where the confrontation over the ad had played out the previous evening. The man I'd more or less rescued stood at the side, straightening a pile of their publications. In the far corner a young woman sat at a tiny desk, writing in a notebook.

The managing editor looked up and smiled as I approached. His badge reminded me of his name, Daryl Hilderman. "Ah, Lady Peacekeeper," he said.

I smiled. "I hope your morning has been calmer so far. Have you gotten yesterday's problem resolved?"

He shrugged. "Passed it up the chain of command. I'm glad it's someone else's problem and not mine."

"It certainly seems peaceful enough around here now. Where is everyone? It isn't usually this quiet."

He laughed. "Ain't that the truth? There's a presentation on some proposed new government regulations downstairs. It could be a major change for a large segment of the juvenile industry. We've got two of our people down there covering it."

"Oh. That would explain it."

His expression grew abruptly more serious. "I have a question. You hold a lot of shows here. Do you feel like there's something different about this one? Not sure what it is, but it seems like something is making a lot of people uneasy. Maybe it's the impending new regulations, but I don't think so. I can't say exactly why, but it feels like there's a lot of tension. Not that there isn't usually at these shows, but there's something different this time. More intense, maybe."

"Among the attendees or the exhibitors?"

"Both, maybe. But I think the exhibitors more. There's always some bad feelings and folks who don't like each other, but there's more than usual. I've already overheard a couple of arguments and the gossip mill is lively. Of course, having a death among the exhibitors is bound to cast a pall."

The young woman in the corner set down her pen and got up. When she came to join us, Daryl introduced her as Felicia Mendez, one of their junior editors. The woman smiled and we shook hands. "I heard the word gossip. Had to get it on this. It's true Lorene Donneywell was hit by a car and killed last night?"

"I'm afraid it is."

"Yikes. I heard the driver didn't stop."

"It was a hit and run, but I believe the police think it was an accident," I answered.

"Wow, that's sad." Felicia looked more curious than dismayed. "Of course, not everyone will be grieving."

"I gather she wasn't popular."

"Not in a lot of quarters. There was always gossip about her."

"Anything particularly juicy?" I asked. "It's not just curiosity. Well, only partly. But I can do my job better if I know what's going on. Or *may be* going on."

Daryl nodded toward a back corner of the booth. Felicia and I moved with him when he sidled that way. He looked up and down the aisle before he spoke. "As far as Lorene is concerned, I got a couple of things, maybe, but again this is all rumor. Not stuff we'd ever publish. And you didn't hear any of this from us, of course."

I grinned. "It's all off the record. I probably don't even know the people involved. But I like to keep up with what's happening."

"You've probably heard Lorene wasn't above using… well, extraordinary means to get what she wanted."

"Lying, cheating, sleeping with whoever to get her way. No, that's not from me. Someone else used those words about her."

"Sounds about right. A lot of people resented her…methods."

"And in the catfight department, there's the thing with our current favorite advertiser," Felicia said.

"Oh, what's that all about?" I asked.

Daryl's eyebrows rose and I thought there might be a mild warning as he looked at Felicia, but she went on. "I'm told that when Janice Langley heard the contract for the Dougal movie tie-ins had gone to Donneywell, she threw a conniption. They'd wined and dined and flattered…and more…and her company thought they had the deal. Janice was fit to be tied when it fell through. They immediately made a deal with Orwell Limited for the Bad Boy Billy series, but everyone knows Billy can't hold a candle to the Dougal Dragon thing. Billy is just a cable TV series where the dragon's going to be a franchise—movie, series, videos, books."

"Wait. That's the woman who was arguing here yesterday afternoon?"

"Janice Langley. She's the product development manager at Carrie Classics. You met her yesterday, I hear."

"I did."

"Then you got a picture of what she's like. Ice-capped volcano. She doesn't get mad. At least not in public. She fumes and fumes and then she gets even. Just ask the people at Markovitz & Company. But you can't. They're out of business, due to her."

"What did she do?"

"Outmaneuvered them for another key contract. Toy and media tie-ins for the "Follow Farley" book series. Markovitz thought they had it tied up until Carrie Classics, driven by Janice Langley, swooped in and snatched it out from under them. Good move for Carrie. They've made a pile on those toys. Very bad for Markovitz. She did it for a couple of other things and the next thing you know Markovitz couldn't compete."

"Wow. What did they do to get her so angry?"

"Not sure, exactly. Something to do with a lawsuit, as I recall. I think Markovitz brought it against Carrie, but I don't know why. And Janice was seriously furious about it."

"The moral of the story being it's dangerous to cross Janice Langley."

"Got it," Felicia said.

"And Lorene Donneywell did." That raised hairs on the back of my neck. I stopped as someone wandered into the booth.

Daryl said, "Excuse me," and went off to talk to the newcomer. I lowered my voice as I asked Felicia, "Any word on whether Janice has threatened Donneywell?"

"Not that I've heard so far. And I think the bad blood between them goes back to well before this."

I would've liked to have pumped her for more on the feud between the late Lorene Donneywell and Janice Langley, but Daryl turned around and called for Felicia to join the conversation he was having.

I reluctantly waved goodbye and wandered away. A few booths down, I stopped to check for messages. Amazingly my phone showed nothing.

The floor still seemed oddly subdued, a condition I hoped could be attributed to the meeting going on in the big ballrooms downstairs. Out of curiosity I went by the Sharpleys booth in the thousands aisle, the one Emilia Grinkoff thought should change spaces with hers.

They used every bit of the area they'd rented. Shelves completely lined the two-booth space, leaving enough room behind the backdrop for a storage area. Spinner racks haphazardly situated turned the rest of the booth into something of a maze. Not a wise idea, in my estimation, to block sight lines in that way. But it wasn't my call, and people did lots of things I thought unwise, impractical, and sometimes totally ridiculous.

Sharpleys' product line was similar to Grinkoff's, though more expansive. Plenty of the same fashion dolls and their accessories lined the shelves and filled racks, but they shared space with other lines of dolls, some much larger ones, and a lot of smaller ones. Some baby dolls elbowed their way into the mix as well.

Given how stuffed the booth was, I didn't see them taking well to any suggestion they exchange places with GlamourThings Inc.

A couple of young men manned the area, but both were engaged with customers, so I didn't try to approach them.

A bit more wandering brought me past booths where I wanted to stop for a better look or just to gape. I'd never been into dolls, but I could entertain myself for hours with colored paper, crayons, scissors, and tape. Much more sophisticated arts and crafts kits were available now. Puzzles came in all sizes, shapes, designs, and even three-dimensional jigsaws that looked seriously challenging.

A booth in the sixteen hundreds aisle stopped me in my tracks for a couple of minutes. PlayBlox was world famous for its interlocking plastic building blocks. They came in so many shapes and colors, you could build almost anything with enough time and patience. The booth displayed a variety of boxed kits providing materials to build castles, towns, vehicles, even spaceships.

To demonstrate the amazing things you could do with the pieces, several large models decorated the area. Most impressive among them was a life-sized replica of a standing Abraham Lincoln. I glanced up at his face. The features were lovingly molded from a mix of small and extra tiny pieces. It wasn't perfect, but he would be recognizable as the sixteenth president, even without the top hat and frock coat fashionable in his day.

An eight-foot-high model of the Washington Monument impressed more for its size and realism than creativity. The fairy castle nearby stood just over three feet, but what it lacked in size, it made up for in intricacy. I counted almost a dozen rounded towers with conical roofs, a square main keep within surrounding walls, and a realistic-looking portcullis in the gate. The towers had those narrow, slit windows, and crenellations topped the walls.

A model of the Brooklyn Bridge sat near a replica of the oddly shaped spaceship from a series of hugely popular science fiction movies. Bins of bricks in the center of the booth invited attendees to try their hands at creating their own masterpieces. I was tempted.

Instead, I headed upstairs. I needed to talk to Janelle about Grinkoff and a couple of other minor issues. I had to wait while she was on the phone, but I used the time to check messages and weed through the emails I'd gotten.

Andrea, the show manager for this event, came in first, so I followed her into her office. I explained Grinkoff's complaint to her.

She rolled her eyes as soon as she heard the name but waited for me to finish, shaking her head through most of my recounting. "That woman. She called a dozen or more times in the last three weeks, telling us she needed a bigger booth. I explained the deadline for applications was past and we were at capacity. Beyond it. I already had five companies on a wait list for space and two for larger booths. I told her I'd put her on the wait list, but it wasn't likely we'd be able to accommodate a change. I checked the invoices and payments to be sure. She paid for one space initially. Nothing after that. But she kept calling back and getting more aggressive about it. I finally had to warn her she wasn't going to get a lot of sympathy or help if she kept being rude to the staff here. I gather she took her complaints to Janelle?"

"She did. And I offered her a sympathetic ear while telling her only that I'd ask about the possibility of a transfer and warning her what you said about the show being full."

"You're a better person than I am," Andrea said. "She wore me out a while back."

"She just started on me this morning. No doubt I'll be joining the worn-out club before the week's over. I have a feeling she won't quit." I turned to check on my boss's status. "I see Janelle's free. I'll tell her about it."

I left Andrea's office and went directly to Janelle's. My boss saw me and signaled me to enter.

We disposed of some of the smaller matters on my list

quickly. Then I told her about Grinkoff's request and my talk with Andrea.

Janelle looked straight at me and said, "You know the answer here. No space. Can't do it. No receipt, no refund. Yadda yadda."

"Yeah. Just warning you to keep the stress-relievers handy."

She offered a crooked smile and tossed me the squishy rubber ball she kept on her desk. I caught it.

"Use whenever you need it," she said. "I find it a great alternative to throwing pots or saying things I'll regret later. And you can get the good coffee down on the floor most days. If it gets more dire than that I'll call in my secret weapon."

"You have a secret weapon?"

"For you," she said. "I've got Scott's number on my phone."

"Oh." I wasn't ready for that. She had a point, though. Scott definitely had some effective de-stressing techniques.

"One other thing," I added. "Though this is sort of un-specific, and maybe not worth bringing up. But I'm—"

Her phone rang and Janelle held up a hand to stop me. She identified herself and listened, then said, "We'll have someone down there in a couple of minutes." She scribbled a number on a sticky note and looked back at me. "You were saying?"

"This isn't too specific, but I've been feeling it a bit my-self. Someone told me today there's a tension around this show he'd never felt before. Couldn't point to anything spe-cific but said there were lots of rumors about bad feelings and ugly possibilities."

Janelle stared at the wall for a moment. "Most shows have their share of bad feelings. But there's nothing we can do about it except try to stay on top of potential trouble and keep it from happening. As much as we can. And speaking of that—" She leaned forward and handed me the note. "Some kind of vandalism at seventeen-forty. I'll see if Scott can meet you there."

SEVEN

Wednesday

SEVENTEEN-FORTY WAS one of the larger booths, comprising eight spaces at the back of the row, occupied by a company that manufactured child-sized, motorized toys kids could drive. A few of them, a tractor large enough for children in the middle grades, and a car and pickup truck sized to fit toddlers, sat on circular platforms in the middle of the booth's floor. Several other variations were displayed on columns. In pride of place at the front of the booth under the glare of spotlights was an empty dais.

At the other end, a theater-like area showed a looping film of children enjoying rides in the company's products. Scott joined me as I entered the booth, and we looked for the person in charge. "I'd've loved something like this when I was a kid," he said, glancing around. His face showed more interest than he usually allowed.

"Me, too." I spotted a man who exuded authority and headed his way. I introduced myself and Scott.

The man, who appeared in his late fifties or early sixties, stood so straight and tall and moved with such precision he had to be ex-military. He introduced himself as Oliver Hanley and signed for us to follow him. We moved to a curtained-off area behind the screen.

Pushed into a corner was another car, a shiny-red min-iature sports model. I had to almost lean over it before I could see the deep scratches gouged into the hood and left side. Scott moved closer as well. His voice sounded rough when he said, "That's...practically sacrilege."

"Indeed," the man said. "It's one of a kind. The only one like it we've made. I argued against bringing it here, but the marketing people convinced me it would be a great draw." He sighed deeply. "Apparently it drew the wrong kind of attention."

"Can it be repaired?" I asked.

The man laid a hand on the damaged hood and brushed gently. "It can be sanded down and refinished. But this was hand-painted." He sounded mournful.

"I'm very sorry." It sounded so inadequate, but I didn't know what else to say. "Do you have any idea who would do this?"

"None at all."

"Do you have any enemies you know of?" Scott asked. "Anyone who'd have a reason to hurt you or your business?"

"Not that I'm aware of." The man continued to study the scratches on the car. "At least not personally. I can't think of anyone. Of course, the company has competitors, and I'm sure some of them are jealous of our success. But I try to run an ethical, above-board business. Integrity is important to me, and it's company policy."

Good in theory, but the policy often got diluted in prac-tice. I'd seen it happen. Scott would understand that as well.

"Did anyone see it happen? Or hear it? Scratching that deeply would make some noise."

"I know. But I've asked the other people here, and none of them heard a thing or saw anyone acting oddly around the display."

Scott asked, "Heather, could you get pictures of the car and the damage?"

I turned on my phone and began taking photos from all angles. I tried to get the best light on the scratches I could.

Scott took out his notebook and pen. "What about the timing? Can we narrow down when this happened?"

"I asked around about that, too. The last time we can verify someone saw the car undamaged was around eleven-thirty this morning."

That jerked me upright. "This morning? This happened during the show? Just hours ago? And no one saw or heard anything?"

Scott looked grim. "When did someone notice the damage?"

"Just before two. Jeff was showing off the cars to a retailer and he saw it. Brought it to my attention as soon as he finished with the customers."

"Was there any time when everyone was gone from the booth?"

"No. There's always someone here."

Scott's eyes narrowed and his expression took on the hard cop-look. "Tell me about your lunch arrangements."

"Ella—my daughter—and I went downstairs to get a bite to eat around twelve-fifteen." He glanced in the direction of a well-dressed, attractively groomed woman in her mid-thirties who was demonstrating controls of the motorized truck to a group of six fascinated men. "We got back before one, I think, and then Jeff went to lunch. He wasn't gone long. The booth has been busy since the show started this morning and none of us wanted to be away long."

My phone buzzed, and a glance showed me it was Janelle, so I moved away to take the call.

"Need you up here as soon as possible," she said. "Is Scott still with you? Ask him to come, too."

I didn't want to interrupt Scott's questions, but Janelle's request had an urgent feel.

Scott was rounding it up anyway. He promised to check out the video feeds for clues and said he'd want to talk to both Jeff and Ella when they were free. Both were still engaged with groups of customers. A glance at my watch showed four-forty. Scott asked if he could come back first thing in the morning to talk to them.

They agreed on that and I held up the phone to show we had another summons. After promising to do everything we could to find the party responsible we headed out.

"What's up?" Scott asked me.

"Don't know." I passed on Janelle's message.

"Don't like the sound of that."

"I know. But about the car... Any chance of figuring out who did it?"

Scott's mouth twisted in a hard grimace as the elevator opened and disgorged us onto the office level. "I don't know. We'll check the video, and I'll talk to Jeff tomorrow. You know he's got to be the prime candidate. I need to find out if he has any motive."

Surprise rushed through me, mixed with dismay, when we walked into Janelle's office and found one of the two guest chairs already occupied by Detective Peter Gilmont. It must have shown on my face because Gilmont grinned wryly as he stood and shook my hand. As usual his reaction to Scott was more enigmatic, but it didn't contain any overt hostility this time. Janelle frowned at me.

As a detective with the Metro D.C. Police Department, Gilmont had investigated a couple of murder cases here during previous shows. He hadn't always been thrilled with my poking into those cases, but he admitted I learned things he never would have. Probably in his late forties, he was still a handsome man, with just a few frown lines on his face and a smattering of gray in the black hair at his temples to show his age. I was pretty sure there was something going on between him and Janelle, but she didn't seem willing to share, and I knew better than to press. They were both divorced and discreet.

I sat down in the other chair and Scott pulled up a stool. Gilmont turned to Janelle. "She's right. My showing up here isn't good news. You haven't told her?"

Janelle grimaced. "Haven't had the chance."

"Told me what?"

Her expression turned worried. "You might've been right about Lorene Donneywell."

"What?"

Gilmont picked it up. "We're treating her death as hit and run murder. It looks like someone ran her down deliberately."

"Oh my God. I'd just convinced myself not every suspicious death I heard about was murder. That sometimes accidents happened."

"And it's true. They do. But it looks like this one wasn't an accident."

"Why not?"

Gilmont shifted in his chair, turning to look at me and Scott. "Witnesses described the car that hit her as moving erratically and shifting lanes at the last moment. The driver appeared to target her, then zipped off so fast no one got the license number. We have a partial number from a surveillance camera. We think it's a Pennsylvania plate. Probably a rental but we're still trying to verify that and identify the company. Otherwise, it's a dark, late-model

SUV. No one got enough look at the driver to even say if it was a man or a woman. The victim died at the scene from massive head trauma."

His lips pressed together in a frown. "Janelle tells me you had some interaction with the victim," Gilmont said. "I'd like to hear your impressions."

"I'm not applying for the fan club." I related my conversation with Lorene Donneywell as best I could remember, and suggested he talk to Jessie. "If she still has any sanity left. The two nieces have been here for a while."

"You don't seem any fonder of the nieces than you were of the aunt."

"They didn't make a great first impression. I suppose you've checked on when they got to D.C. and what they did after they arrived?"

"Working on it. We've established one of them—Angelina, I think?—landed at Reagan National from La-Guardia earlier today, took a cab to her hotel, and checked in at one-fifteen. That much is verified."

"It's not an alibi, though," I said. "She could've driven from New York to here yesterday and gone back last night. Could even have grabbed a few hours of sleep before the flight."

Gilmont's mouth crooked. "True, but premature."

Heat rose in my cheeks. "Speculation."

"We determined the hit and run was a likely murder this morning after reviewing witness statements and video. We're still running down relatives and information about the victim. From what you've said, it sounds like she might've had enemies?"

I laughed, though the rather bitter, cynical sound surprised me. "I think that's a safe bet. Even her assistant, the girl working with her at the booth, didn't like her very much."

Janelle flipped a pen around in her fingers, something she frequently did when thinking. "What do you need from us?"

"Access to the show floor, so we can talk to anyone who turns up as involved, for one thing. I promise discretion."

"You already have a staff pass you can use at any time."

"I know, but I wanted you to know we would be around and talking to people. More than that, though, I want Heather to keep her ear to the ground and give me a heads-up about any gossip or leads related to Lorene Donneywell. My gut is telling me there could be a business tie-in on the murder, and she'll hear more about it than I ever will."

I was so stunned it took a moment to respond. The detective had warned me off prying into previous cases. "You want me to ask around about her?"

Gilmont's relaxed posture went noticeably stiffer. "Not overtly. Just stay tuned to the gossip. Nudge it if you want but don't push it. Give us a lead or two if you get any and we'll follow up."

"All right. I can do that."

Janelle's expression went stern. "You will not take any chances with this. I don't want a repeat of what happened in this office a few weeks ago."

I could still feel the chills running down my back as I'd barricaded myself in Janelle's office, praying a murderer wouldn't be able to break down the door. "Neither do I."

I turned to the detective. "As a matter of fact, I did hear something earlier today that may be relevant." Each of the other three in the room watched me as I related the part of the conversation I'd had with Daryl and Felicia earlier today concerning Janice Langley's reaction to the loss of

the Dougal Dragon license. I added in my impressions of
the woman from the confrontation at the magazine's booth
the previous day.

Gilmont's eyebrows rose as I continued the story about
her reaction to other losses. He laughed wryly as I finished.
"You're already handing me a possible suspect, complete
with motive and history."

"Nope, just repeating gossip. What you do with it is your
business."

Scott rolled his eyes.

JANELLE HAD SPARED me the need to stay for the show's opening dinner party that evening, since she planned to go herself to represent the Center. I wondered if she would be
taking Gilmont with her. He'd been wearing a nice suit.
The event would give him a chance to do his own assess-
ment of some of the big players in the industry.

As usual Scott drove me home, and we stopped for dinner at a favorite place for fast, casual dining.

I was feeling down. "This show is usually so much
fun," I said over a southwestern salad. "I mean—toys. And
games. The demos are great and there are always neat new
things to see. Yeah, there's usually some bickering and bad
feeling about who got which contract or award for hot-
test new toy or best new gadget. But this feels different.
Darker. Like there's a cloud over the whole thing. It kind
of scares me."

"It should." I glanced at him, surprised by the force he
put behind the words. But then he looked abashed. "Sorry.
I'm feeling some of the same and it worries me, too. That bit
of gossip you shared with Gilmont didn't help. The gun, the
vandalism of the car. A sense of building pressure among
the exhibitors. It could all add up to trouble."

I reached for his hand and held it. "Or it may come to nothing at all. We might be over-reacting or being hyper-sensitive based on past experiences."

He squeezed my fingers and it felt entirely different from the way Janice Langley had done it the day before. His strength was tempered to just the right force to convey reassurance without being painful. "Maybe we are. But it doesn't hurt to stay on guard for trouble."

EIGHT

Thursday

THURSDAY MORNING GOT off to a mostly normal start. No notes from Janelle waited on my desk, no critical emails red-flagged my inbox, not even an urgent message blinked on the landline phone. In fact, Janelle hadn't arrived by the time I headed downstairs to the show floor. Nothing delayed the dreaded visit to Emilia Grinkoff.

I wandered the show floor first, making it a point to pass by the Carrie Classics spot in the eleven hundred aisle. It was a center end booth taking up six spaces. Their product line overlapped with Donneywell's but was more extensive, including a variety of animals and dolls. A six-foot-tall stuffed critter that looked like a cross between a monkey and a kangaroo, wearing a cowboy hat and boots, was featured front and center of the booth. A huge banner over it identified it as "Bad Boy Billy." I remembered Daryl or Felicia saying something about the tie-in being a sort of a consolation prize for losing the Dougal the Dragon rights. The dragon had looked much more appealing to me. Honestly, I found it hard to envision any parent wanting Bad Boy Billy hanging around their house, but then I don't have kids, so what do I know?

I looked around for Janice Langley or Sam Schmidt, but

only two men I'd never met manned the booth. One was demonstrating a line of dolls to a group of buyers. The other stepped toward me.

He was a shade under six feet tall, young—very young, in fact, no more than early twenties—blond, impeccably groomed, with features that worked better on Janice than on him. But his pleasant expression and unforced smile made up for a lot. He held out a hand and the grin broadened when he noticed my name tag, which doesn't happen a lot. Or *was* it my ID he was looking at?

Whichever, he quickly moved his gaze upward again. "Hey! How's it going? Ross Langley."

I shook his hand as I told him my name and position in return. "I stopped by to see if everything was okay here. I met Janice Langley a couple of days ago when there was a bit of a crisis over a magazine ad. I hope everything was resolved to her satisfaction."

His mouth twitched. "You met my mother? In a crisis? Then I suppose it's too late to make a good first impression."

I must have looked shocked. He laughed. "She knows. She's heard it before."

Which didn't mean she'd appreciate it, but if the kid was working in his mother's company, they must have some understanding. "She's not here right now?"

He shook his head. "Off working some new deal. You've got to stay ahead of the curve if you want to succeed in this business."

I wondered if she was actually talking to Pete Gilmont right then, but he likely wouldn't want to share if it were the case. Instead, I followed up on the business deal notion. "I understand your mother's good at that."

He grinned. "Yup. Two big new product intros for this

show. Bad Boy Billy and The World Travelers doll set." He pointed out both with a sweep of his arm. "Both are up for "Plaything of the Year" awards and we're betting both will win their categories. Let me show you."

He led the way to a shelf at the side of the booth, selected several dolls from The World Travelers grouping, and pointed out how each was dressed in an outfit appropriate for the country they visited. Each had small accessories—suitcases, backpacks, hats, gloves, shoes, etc.—to go with their garb. His smile remained in place as he did this, though it showed subtle signs of strain.

I was getting a weird vibe from this young man. Cute and friendly as he was, there was something beneath the overt charm I couldn't quite pin down. It almost felt like he was running a private joke at my expense—or thought he was, anyway—or there was something deeper going on and he wanted to tease me with it.

Or maybe he was a good salesman, and I was being affected by the gloomy atmosphere.

"The dolls are very interesting." Mostly true, even if I'd never been much of a doll person as a kid. "Very educational. I'm glad to hear things are going well, since I gather she's had some disappointments recently." I probably should've resisted but I wanted to get his reaction.

His mouth worked, trying to keep the grin in place. His shrug was disarmingly ingenuous. "That's how it goes in this business. In most businesses, I bet. You win some. You lose some. Some get snatched right out from under you."

"The Dragon thing?"

"So she said. And when Mama Mia speaks, everyone agrees. If they're smart."

Definitely a weird vibe. "It's hard to imagine someone

could snatch anything out from under her. She seems very on top of things."

"No sh—I mean, no joke. But when you play any game, you're going to lose a round occasionally."

"Truth. So, this is a family business?" I asked. Perfectly innocent question, right? Not exactly.

Ross's face lost the practiced smile fast, replaced by a tight, narrow-eyed frown that lasted only a moment before he smoothed out his expression again. "Maybe. It should be. It's complicated." He started to say something else and clamped down on it.

I didn't really want to put my foot into that swamp. "Okay."

We were both saved from having to find a different topic of conversation by the arrival of another group of customers. Ross said, "See you later," as he moved off to greet the newcomers. I didn't hear a sigh of relief, but I was betting he'd heaved one.

I walked around for a bit, puzzling over Ross Langley and his relationship with his mother. But my unconscious brain apparently guided my footsteps, since I soon found myself facing the six hundred aisle, location of the GlamourThings booth. I jerked myself back into Assistant to the Director mode and squared my shoulders as I approached.

Emilia Grinkoff had a group of customers with her, crowding the limited space in the tent, so I backed off and let out a relieved breath. Prematurely.

As I turned, a distinguished-looking, gray-haired man beckoned me over to his booth across the aisle. The company produced custom-printed books that would include a specified child as a character, which seemed a neat idea to me. But pushing his product wasn't what the gentleman had in mind.

After introducing himself, he said, "You're on the staff of the Market Center, aren't you? Mary at Hamilton-Sawyer pointed you out yesterday. We're hoping you can help us out. That booth is driving us nuts."

I told him who I was and my position. I didn't have to turn to look to know which space he referred to. "What's the problem?"

He looked up at the ceiling for a moment. "What isn't the problem? That maddening music… They've got it turned down right now but at times they play it loud. And the arguments. Very loud, too. It's distracting when we're trying to talk to customers."

"Arguments? With customers?"

"Oh, no. They're all professional with the customers. At least as far as I can tell. No. The woman and man who run the booth."

This was news. "I didn't know there was anyone in the booth beside Ms. Grinkoff."

He looked toward it, and his expression drew into a frown. "There's a man works there with her. He's not particularly friendly. Doesn't wave or smile or say hello when he goes by. Not that she's very sociable either, but sometimes she says hello. He never says anything. Acts like the rest of us don't exist. But, let me tell you, he and that woman have it out at times. It's disturbing."

"Can you tell what they're arguing about?"

"Never can make out the words but haven't really tried. Not sure it's even all English."

I kept my dismay out of sight. This was a complication I didn't need.

"Oh, and those things on their tent keep flapping over on their neighbors' displays. Glad I'm not one of them, but I know people on both sides are annoyed about it."

"Okay. I'll see what I can do."

The customers were leaving the tent, though the process was slowed when Grinkoff had a few more words for them as they went.

Her smile broadened when she saw me approaching. "You've got good news for me?"

Something in that smile and her stance told me she knew I didn't, and she was ready for battle. I braced myself—mentally, at least. "I'm afraid not. I warned you it wasn't likely we could move you, but I did inquire about it. The thing is, we don't have any place for you, and we can't ask other exhibitors to move from their current locations."

She waited a moment to respond. "This is bad business. You're at least going to offer a refund for this mistake?"

"The only records of transactions we have from you are the original request for a single space and payment for it. Our call logs show you requested a change very late, long after the deadline, long after all booth assignments were issued. We put you on a waiting list. Unfortunately, there were no cancellations so we couldn't fulfill the request, and you were never promised a larger space or billed for it, nor did you pay for it. So there's nothing to refund."

Her facial muscles tightened, and her cheeks flushed red.

I held up a hand. "But we are willing to give you first option for a larger booth for next year and a discount on the cost." Nobody had actually authorized me to do that, but the Center would honor my word on it.

She huffed in a breath and let it out sharply. "I don't know if we'll be coming back next year after the way we've been treated this year. But if we do, I'll certainly take you up on it. It's the least you can do after this…this…fiasco."

I resisted saying it would be no skin off our noses if she didn't come back. "I'm sorry you feel that way, but we do the best we can to accommodate all requests, as long as they're submitted in a timely fashion." I managed it with a straight face, and I think I kept all hint of irony out of the words. "But there's another issue we need to talk about. We try not to interfere with any of our exhibitors' displays, and we give everyone a lot of latitude. But we do have to draw a line when the display or noise interferes with other exhibitors' business. We've had complaints about the noise level coming from your booth. Apparently, you sometimes play music quite loudly, and it makes it difficult for your neighbors to hold conversations with their customers. I hope you'll keep it lower for the rest of the show." I decided not to get into the arguments right now. If I could get them to turn down the music, maybe she'd get the message on the arguments as well. Maybe.

An odd tingle prickled my neck, the subliminal message your mind sends that someone is watching you. I turned my head and caught a brief glimpse of a man's face peeking out from the slot between the back and side canvas flaps of the tent. He withdrew quickly when I looked his way, pulling the flaps together to hide his face. In the quick glimpse I'd gotten, I'd guess him at late forties, with dark hair and a dark mustache. I glanced down, A pair of large feet in black leather lace-up shoes showed in the four-inch-gap between the floor and the bottom of the canvas. He still stood there, no doubt listening to the conversation.

Meanwhile Grinkoff's face grew redder under the thick layer of make-up. "They're just jealous we draw more attention than they do."

"Maybe so. But it doesn't matter. I need you to keep the noise lower."

She grumbled incoherently, under her breath, for a moment. "This show is terrible. Can't do anything."

"I'm sorry." I tried for my most placating smile. "We try not to constrict our exhibitors, but we have to balance the needs of all. And legal and safety considerations, of course." I'm not sure what moved me to add the last bit. I looked back to where I'd seen the feet of the mysterious listener, but they were gone.

Grinkoff huffed out. "Well, I'll do my best to comply."

I thanked her as sweetly as I could manage and left.

Amazingly there were no messages on my phone, and I'd taken care of everything I knew about.

I'm not sure what masochistic tendency urged me to go by the Donneywell booth to see how everyone was coping there.

NINE

Thursday

JESSIE SAT AT a small table near the side of the booth with a stack of brochures and sell sheets, but I almost didn't recognize her. I blinked twice at the transformation in the young woman. Gone were the unkempt locks pulled ruthlessly back into a messy ponytail, replaced by rippling, glossy brown waves. Makeup widened her sleepy eyes, and lipstick brightened her olive coloring. The last time I'd seen her, slumped shoulders, a baggy shirt, and a lazy frown emphasized what appeared to be a gloomy disposition. Today she sat straight and wore a red and black patterned dress that showed off nice curves. Two-inch-heeled black pumps emphasized shapely legs.

I tried not to stare. She looked so different. Maybe it was the show starting—but no, she hadn't looked like this yesterday morning.

I told myself to stop gawking. "You look fabulous," I said as I approached her. I kept it low, though, since fifteen feet away, Olivia was talking to a potential buyer about a rack of stuffed dragons.

Jessie looked around and shrugged. "Time to prove I could."

While I was still puzzling out what she meant, Angelina

Donneywell came up to us. "Miss—" She looked at my badge. "McNeil. Heather. We appreciate you taking care of the badges. This is proving very interesting."

Jessie's eyebrows rose, and a strange, wry smile twisted her lips, but she didn't say anything.

The overhead lighting on the show floor didn't flatter anybody, but it somehow made the blue streaks in Angelina's hair glow. On the other hand, it didn't enhance a sallow complexion set off by too much blue eyeshadow and purple-hued lipstick. The denim leggings and striped tunic were more casual than most participants would consider appropriate for a show like this.

Apparently, this was how Angelina rolled. The woman who wore vivid blue stripes in her hair didn't care about dressing professionally. But she did seem friendly enough.

"How's it going here?" I looked from Angelina to Jessie to direct the question at both of them. Jessie scanned the area and her gaze rested on Olivia and the buyer for a moment before turning toward Angelina.

Angelina smiled brightly before saying, "Oh, it's great! It looks like we're getting lots of orders for the dolls."

"Dolls?"

"You know, those stuffed animals. The dragons."

"They're getting lots of attention," Jessie added.

Verifying her words, a group of two men and a woman stopped to admire the huge stuffed dragon Jessie repaired a couple of days ago. I couldn't even see the tear, so she'd done a good job. I heard one newcomer say, "Dougal" and the others echo it in recognition. Jessie watched Angelina, waiting for her to move toward them. When Angelina just stayed there and looked, Jessie stood and went to greet them.

I didn't hide my surprise well, I guess. Angelina gave

me a sad, wry smile. "I'm not good at selling things. So, I leave it to them."

"What's your strong point?"

She grinned. "Ideas. I'm great at ideas. I already have a few thoughts on how we can improve this booth."

I looked around at the exhibit and didn't see anything I thought obviously needed upgrading. "What would you do?

"Oh." Her face lit with enthusiasm. "First, I'd play up the dragon angle since that's our big product right now. Maybe turn part of the backdrop into a castle scene with a dragon flying around it. It's a big movie tie-in so we can probably get stills from the production company. Hang a canopy over it with a medieval flair. Turn some of the display racks into stone towers, that kind of thing."

Her ideas had merit. I'd seen stranger booth displays designed to support product branding. A couple of years ago one toy company built an entire log cabin encompassing most of their booth when they introduced a new line of wood construction sets.

While I considered her ideas, Olivia Donneywell finished and said goodbye to the group of buyers. She came toward us and nodded to me. She wore an expensive power suit that stretched every seam nearly to bursting and sported a formidable glower as she approached. "Is there a problem, Miss McNeil?" she asked. "It's already been an appalling morning."

"I'm sorry to hear it. What's happened?"

She shut her eyes and shook her head. "I spent more than an hour with the detective who's investigating Lorene's death. And he acted like I was their prime suspect, asking me questions about where I was Tuesday night and Wednesday morning. Wanted me to prove I was where I said I was. He kept demanding to know how I felt about my aunt, whether I was angry at her or hated her or jealous of her. It was insulting! Why would I want to hurt Lorene? She was good to me. He took me away from here for too long."

Nice to know what her priorities were.

"I talked to him, too," Angelina said. "He asked me all those same questions. And he really jumped on it when I told him I was at home Tuesday night and all alone so I couldn't prove anything. I'm sure he thinks I snuck down here early and ran down Aunt Lorene. He made me feel guilty even though I know I'm not!"

"He's just doing his job," I said.

"His job is to harass people and keep them from doing important work during a show that can make or break your business?" Olivia raised her voice then hushed it when she looked around and saw someone across the aisle staring at her.

Angelina rolled her eyes. "His job is to figure out who killed Aunt Lorene, and I, for one, hope he does it."

"He's good at it," I assured her.

"Yes, but is he looking at all the other people here who hated Lorene?" Olivia asked. "Or is he just focusing on family?"

"Other people here hated Lorene?" Yes, I already knew it was true, but I wanted to get their slant on it.

Olivia glanced over at Jessie and turned back to me. "Lorene was…determined. When she wanted something, she went for it, guns blazing. She'd use everything at her disposal, every weapon she had to succeed. That's how she built the business. Of course, it didn't make her popular with some people."

"Business rivals?"

"Mostly."

"Anyone in particular you can think of?"

She sighed and shook her head. "No one, specifically."

Angelina looked at her. "There was the one she called the witch queen. She really didn't like her."

"I guess she didn't. Do you know who she meant?"

"Nope. But they'd gone head-to-head over licensing deals on some products. This other woman had won a few rounds, and Lorene didn't think it was a level playing ground."

"You don't know the company this person is with?"

"No, sorry."

"Do you know what Lorene thought had happened to influence the deals?" I tried to sound like I had no idea.

"Not sure."

Jessie finished up with the group she had been talking to and returned to join us. She held up a completed order form. "Small regional chain. They want two hundred of the twenty-inch Dougals and fifty of the forty-inch ones."

"That's great!" Angelina sounded excited. Olivia's "very good" was more muted.

"Good sales job," I said. "We were talking about Lorene's murder. I wondered if there were business acquaintances who might have hated or resented her enough to harm her. Angelina said there was one person Lorene called the witch queen, but she doesn't know who that is."

One of Jessie's perfectly groomed eyebrows rose, and she chewed her lip for a moment before answering. "I don't either, exactly. If it's who I suspect, she got to a couple of valuable licensing possibilities before Lorene did. Before Lorene even knew it was available, in one case. That ticked her off."

Jessie met my sharp glance with a steady one of her own. Not a challenge, exactly, but interest, more than she'd shown in anything so far. The other two women looked at her with surprise and curiosity. "You know who the 'witch queen' is?" Olivia asked.

Jessie shook her head. "Just a suspicion and I'd rather not talk about it." A man and a woman approached the booth right then and looked over the dragons. Without checking with either of the Donneywells, Jessie went over and engaged them.

Olivia's gaze followed Jessie for a moment and her brow wrinkled. "What do you suppose that was all about?" she asked softly.

"She wanted us to know she has a suspicion. I'll try to follow up with her on it later. In the meantime, if you have any idea who might have wanted to harm Lorene, please do let Detective Gilmont know. He'll check it all out, I promise."

"That's what I'm worried about," Olivia said. "He seems so focused on family. Which means us." She glanced at Angelina. "I guess it does make sense. We're the ones who benefit."

"It's a strong motive," I agreed.

"But honestly, I wasn't ready to take over this company. I have another project I've been working on and it's going to stretch me to keep up with both."

Angelina rolled her eyes. "Isn't it time you gave up on the fancy sock business? It isn't going anywhere, even with all the cash Lorene pumped into it to bail you out. This company is more profitable than DonneySocks will ever hope to be."

Olivia straightened up and glared at her cousin. "Those were loans and I've paid her back. And the business is looking up."

"Paid her back some of it. What about all the money she invested in putting Kevin through college?"

"That was her choice. She wanted to help. And don't be so high and mighty. You weren't above begging for help yourself. The incident in Hartford, for instance."

"Wasn't my fault. Aunt Lorene understood."

Their voices were gaining volume. One of the people with Jessie, perusing the dragons catalog, looked up sharply.

"Getting loud, ladies," I said.

Angelina giggled and said, "Sorry. I'll try to keep it down…"

As she was speaking a fuss broke out nearby, marked by increasingly loud voices and cries of "Hey!" and "What the heck?" Shoes squeaked and clacked as a group of people approached. A noise sounded like a dog's yip. I turned to look and as I did, a small, four-legged ball of white fur scooted between my legs, rushed across the booth, circled around the huge dragon figure, and scurried down the aisle toward the back of the hall, ears flapping and tail wagging.

"What was that?" I asked, loudly, into the air.

"I think it was a dog," Angelina offered. "I didn't think pets were allowed in here."

"They're not."

A small group of people chased after the dog, gathering followers as they went. I excused myself to the Donneywells and turned to join them. I wanted to know why a dog was running around the show floor and how it got in. My shoes weren't best suited for chasing after runaway animals, but the same was true of most of the people around me as well. Voices called for the animal to "Stop" and "Come here," while heels clacked or squeaked during the pursuit.

Up ahead, the fuss grew louder and sharper, with people yelling, items clattering, and more, louder yips from the object of the chase. At a booth on the far end of the eight hundred aisle, people gathered in a crowd, where I guessed they had the animal cornered. I had to push through the onlookers to get in place to see what was going on. When a couple of individuals didn't want to move, I yelled, "Center personnel, let me through."

That gained me enough clearance to push my way to the front of the group, with a couple of feet between myself and a group of two women and a man, trying to coax the wayward dog out from under a skirted table. One woman was on her hands and knees, despite the tight dress she wore. She inched aside the drape enclosing the table. A low growl answered her efforts.

"Come on out, doggie," she said, holding her hand, palm up, in his direction. I couldn't see the animal, but the table shook and drapery shifted, plus another warning growl came from the shadows.

"What the hell is going on? How did that animal get in here?" A heavy-set, balding man approached. He appeared to go with the booth, which featured infant and toddler toys. "You said you're with the Center?" He looked my way. "Do something about this. And make sure it doesn't do any business here."

Any business? It took me a moment, which led to one of those, *Oh hell, no* moments.

I stalked up to the three people nearest the table. "Is that your dog under there?"

The woman trying to coax the dog out looked up at me briefly. "No. He ran through my booth."

A tall, thin woman at the far end of the chasing group took a step toward me and said, so softly I could barely make out the words, "He's mine." She looked to be on the verge of tears. "He's my emotional support animal." I glanced at her name tag. Emma Simmons was an exhibitor, listed as a representative of "Tommy's Toy Box."

The growling grew louder and the table shook harder. I turned away from her for the moment. The man who ran the booth grabbed a spinner rack of baby rattles and pulled it off the table, setting it on the floor nearby. A stack of brochures went flying, scattering across the booth and fluttering into the next one.

"What's his name?" the woman reaching under the booth yelled.

"PooBear," Emma said, again so quietly only those of us close to her could hear.

"His name's 'PooBear,'" I relayed, then said to Emma, "Come up here and call him yourself. He'll probably respond better to you." While she stepped forward, I sent off quick texts to Security and Maintenance. I hoped we wouldn't need either, but I wasn't betting on it.

Emma crouched down and spoke softly while the other woman backed away. I scanned the scene and realized the dog was basically cornered if enough people blocked off all possible ways he could run.

While Emma tried to lure PooBear out of hiding, I turned to the gathered group. "Guys," I said, addressing all of them in the loudest voice I could. "Form a circle around the table. Not too tight, but don't leave enough room for him to squeeze between anyone's legs." I expected to have to coax and cajole people into place, but in fact everyone agreed and took positions in a circle around the table where the dog hid. I walked around the inside of the ring while the original woman and Emma continued to call to the creature. A couple of people were too close. and others left too much room between them. With minor adjustments, they had a solid containment field around the dog's retreat.

PooBear stopped growling, possibly on hearing his mistress's voice, but when she tried to reach under the table to him, he barked sharply. Emma leaned back. "That's not a good doggie," she crooned. "Come on, PooBear. Come to mama."

PooBear wasn't in a co-operative mood. Emma reached into a pocket and pulled out a dog biscuit. "Cookie, Poo-Bear," she said. "PooBear wants a cookie?"

A black nose surrounded by white fur emerged from the darkness under the table and sniffed at the treat Emma held out. The dog inched forward, huffing loudly enough I could hear it over the chatter from the circle of people, and the crowd gathered beyond them. Emma slowly withdrew the cookie to lure PooBear out far enough that she could grab his collar.

The creature was mostly a ball of white fuzz. I knew nothing about dogs except what I'd learned during pet product shows, and I had no idea what breed or mix this one was. But it was fast and sly. As Emma reached for his collar, the dog twisted, snatched the biscuit from her hand, and slid back under the table.

One woman on the other side of the circle had the good sense to flip up the drapery, so the dog no longer had a protected retreat. While the fuzzball stared at us, crunching the stolen biscuit, he failed to notice the woman behind, who had moved forward, with the two men at her side shifting alongside so the containment didn't break in the process. With no warning, she dove forward and got both hands under the dog's belly. PooBear yipped and squirmed as she lifted him toward her chest, but the woman held on and brought him over to Emma.

The animal wriggled and growled during the transfer.

"Do not let go of him," I whispered to Emma. Then, more loudly, I thanked everyone for their help with catching the dog. Most took the hint and wandered off. I looked around at those remaining and spotted both Scott and Mark. Mark had a maintenance cart at the ready.

The men approached, though neither looked at the other. Both worked for the Market Center, but friendly co-workers they were not. That was mostly my fault, in a roundabout way. Mark has had a crush on me since he started working here eighteen months ago, but he convinced himself I turned down his date requests because I didn't date fellow employees. No, I never told him so. He decided it on his own. Then Scott started working here a few months ago and we began dating soon thereafter. Yes, it was awkward.

I told Emma, "Come with me," and moved toward the aisle.

As I passed Mark, I said, "Sorry to ask this, but please help them clean up and make sure the dog didn't leave any remnants in the booth, of any variety."

He wrinkled his nose and frowned at me but pushed the cart into the booth. I nodded for Scott to come with us.

"We can't allow animals other than certified service animals on the show floor," I said to Emma. "Is PooBear certified?"

Based on his free-wheeling excursion around the exhibit hall and lack of the usual service vest, I suspected not. We'd had certified service animals at various shows, and they were always well behaved. "No," she admitted. "I want to get him certified, but he needs some additional training to qualify."

"I'm sorry, but I'll have to ask you to take him out."

She gulped back a sob. "I'm sorry he caused so much disruption. PooBear isn't usually so hyper."

"Maybe he isn't used to so many people around," Scott said.

Emma jumped and turned to look at him.

"I'm sorry," I said. "This is Scott. He works for the Center, too." I didn't tell her he was Security. She would probably figure it out for herself, but I didn't want to make a point of it.

"Oh. I don't know. He comes to the store with me all the time."

"But those are familiar surroundings," Scott answered as we steered her toward the exit. "This place is big and noisy and strange to him. It probably freaked him out."

"Maybe," she said. "I guess I didn't think about that when I brought him."

"Speaking of bringing him, how did you get him in?" I asked. "Our monitors at the doors are supposed to check for pets."

A flush rose on her cheeks. "He was wrapped in a blanket when I came in. They might have assumed he was a baby."

Scott grimaced. They weren't supposed to let small children in either, but his tone was gentle when he said, "I believe Heather knows a pet-sitting service nearby that does a good job."

"I do, and I'll be happy to give you a referral. The owner is very careful about who she accepts, but if you tell her I sent you, she'll take PooBear on. She's good and she'll give PooBear the royal treatment."

It wasn't the first time I'd given this speech. I pulled out one of my business cards from a pocket of the show badge and wrote the phone number on the back before handing it to Emma.

By that point, we'd reached the door. Emma looked hesitant as she accepted the card from me. "I don't know... I really need him nearby to function." She shook and looked close to tears.

"This place is just down the street. You can visit him

any time you want or need to," I assured her. "They don't mind at all."

Emma bit her lip. "I'll think about it." She turned and walked away. I breathed out a long sigh.

"She probably does need the dog for support," Scott said, watching the woman disappear into the crowd in the lobby, a thoughtful frown creasing his features. "She seems to be one of those people who walk a fine line when it comes to functioning."

"I know and I understand. I feel bad for her, too, but it's center policy that only certified service animals are allowed, except under special conditions. We sometimes bend the rules a bit for the pet products shows, but we have pretty strict standards."

Scott gave me a surprised look. "You're preaching to the choir when it comes to enforcing rules with gray areas and hard decisions."

"I forgot. Right."

"But that doesn't mean there's no place for compassion."

"I know. I sometimes have trouble with where the lines are."

"Don't we all. Have you had lunch yet?" he asked. "I haven't, and I'm starving. Assuming there aren't any other crises demanding your attention?"

I pulled out my phone. Blessedly no texts. One missed call from a friend that I'd return later. I was stunned to realize it was after one. I'd totally lost track of the time, but my stomach rumbled to remind me it wanted fuel. "Nothing," I said. "Let's go. I want to hear what you've learned today."

TEN

Thursday

"I HATE TO disappoint you," Scott said, after we'd gotten wraps from a vendor and taken them to a quiet table in a back corner. The food court area wasn't empty, but it wasn't as crowded as it likely had been an hour ago. "I haven't learned much. I spent an hour going over tape this morning and I didn't find any clues to the vandalism at Hanley. It's bizarre since there had to be some noise, but no one ever seemed to notice anything going on."

"Did you talk to the other guy—the one who wasn't there when we were?"

"Jeff? I did. And I didn't get any kind of malicious vibes from him. Just the opposite. He's thrilled with his job and the products and enthusiastic about the company. He seemed genuinely upset when I asked about the damage to the car."

I sighed. "You have good instincts about people. Where does that leave us?"

Scott chewed a bit of his wrap for a moment. His phone buzzed. He pulled it out, glanced at it, and pushed it back into its holder. "I don't know. I don't like it, though. There's an ugliness about it that's disturbing."

"Can't argue. I don't know if my morning was any more

productive…aside from chasing runaway dogs." I told him about my various conversations.

Scott seemed most interested in the talk with Ross Langley. "I wouldn't be happy to know one of my kids said things like that about me."

"True, but he said his mother knew. Said it in a way that suggested she didn't mind."

"You believe it?"

I considered. "Not enough information yet. I got an odd vibe from him I can't really put my finger on. But if you'd met her—"

My phone buzzed and I glanced at it. "Janelle. I'd better take it."

Scott nodded. We were both still on duty.

"Sorry to spring this on you," Janelle said, "But one of the people Pete Gilmont talked to today is royally peeved about it and telling all her neighbors what a horrible operation this is, how incompetent we all are, and threatening to sue the Center for… I'm not sure what, but I'm sure she can think of a few things. She didn't come to me directly with that. Two of her neighbors were alarmed enough to call up here to tell us. Do you think you could try to talk to her? Find out what exactly her grievance is and if it's something we should take seriously."

"Sounds like fun… Not."

"No. And I understand if you can't get far. You know not to make promises we can't keep, but you do have a gift for calming disturbed people."

"'Blessed are the peacemakers'?" I quoted.

"Underpaid, anyway, I'm sure," Janelle answered. "Just scope it out."

"I'm so remembering that at review time. Okay. Who am I scoping?"

A short pause ensued, and I pictured Janelle reading the name from a sticky note on her desk. "A Janice Langley. Carrie Classics. Booth number…"

"Eleven-twenty-two."

"Oh. I thought the name rang a bell. You've talked to her."

"Sadly, yes."

"And you're not looking forward to this."

"Understatement." I let my head fall forward a bit as I grimaced. "She's difficult. That's another understatement."

"Maybe I should come down and talk to her."

"You may need to, but let's not start there," I said. "I'll talk to her and get a read."

Janelle thanked me and ended the call.

"Speaking of devils." I looked at Scott. "Apparently Ross Langley's mother took exception to being interviewed by Pete Gilmont. She's now raging about it to anyone who'll listen and threatening to sue. Not sure what for but she can probably think up something. I need to go find out how serious she is and what it will take to calm her down."

Scott's face went into "cop mode," his expression hardening into sternness. It didn't make him any less attractive—to me, anyway—but I expected it could be off-putting to others. "Maybe I should go with you."

I shook my head. "Wave a red flag in front of a raging bull? Uh-uh. This is going to be tricky, though, because I did point Gilmont in her direction. But I only told him there was bad blood between her and the victim… I wouldn't mind if you would stay not too far away and listen for a ping."

"You've got it. Are you finished?" He looked at the bit of food on the table in front of me.

I wasn't, but my appetite had just vacated the premises.

"Done." I smushed the paper containing the last few bites of the wrap I no longer wanted. I took a final drink from the soda cup. We dumped our trash and headed back to the show floor. At the eleven hundred row I pointed to the booth on the other side of the long transverse aisle. "Why don't you wait around the other side of thirteen hundred. I'll buzz you if needed."

He nodded and we split up. I headed straight up the aisle, squaring my shoulders as I went. I'd handled plenty of conflicts as part of my job, and I usually enjoyed figuring out ways to settle disputes and resolve contentious issues. But I always had a bit of concern when dealing with angry people, especially when they were likely angry with me. Usually, I could calm them and work on a solution to whatever bothered them, but occasionally the person was so far beyond rational thinking or functioning there was no reasoning with them. A couple of times I'd needed Security to intervene to remove those people. I'd had my job threatened more than once, sometimes maybe even with reason, though this wasn't that kind of situation.

Janice Langley and Sam Schmidt were both in the Carrie Classics booth when I approached it. I didn't see Ross Langley. No buyers hung around either. Janice straightened stacks of flyers and Schmidt sucked on a cup of coffee. Both looked up as I approached. Schmidt smiled. Janice didn't. She stalked toward me.

"You were the one told the detective I had it in for Lorene Donneywell. Who else here would know? You had no right. I'll sue the Market Center for defamation and libel. How dare you make up stories like that about me?"

I held up a hand. "Whoa. First, I don't know where you're getting your information, but I never told anyone you *had it in* for Lorene Donneywell. If by 'the detective'

you mean Detective Gilmont, he asked me if I knew of anyone here who didn't like Lorene, and your name came up
on the list. It's common knowledge you and she were not
BFFs. However, you're certainly not the only person who
fits the category. I gather she wasn't the most popular person in the industry."

"You've got that right. She could be a first-rate bitch
and didn't care who knew it or who got trampled under
her ambition. But it doesn't mean I wanted to kill her."
The woman's face twisted into a frown. "Okay, there were
times when I did want to kill her. But I didn't. Too messy
and dangerous. I value my own life and freedom too much
to do something so stupid. I admit I wanted to beat her at
her own game, though. And sometimes I did. That was a
lot more satisfying."

Schmidt joined us and gave a crooked smile which
showed all too clearly the effort it took to produce it. "Miss
McNeil." He nodded at me, then looked at Janice. "Have
you settled down?" he asked her.

"Not much. I'm still hugely insulted by the way that detective acted like I'd murdered Lorene." She drew a breath
before turning a furious gaze my way, and jabbed a finger
in my direction, the long, scarlet nail aimed firmly at my
chest. "And I'm not happy you told the detective about me.
You had no right."

Schmidt shook his head at Janice. "She not only has the
right, she had an obligation. This is a murder investigation.
Very serious business, and the police need all the information they can get to help them catch the person responsible."

"The Center and its people need to keep themselves out
of this," Janice insisted. "It's not their business."

"It becomes our business when one of our exhibitors

is murdered, and there's a good chance the murderer is at this show."

Schmidt's brow crinkled. "Why would that be? Isn't it possible it was just some random hit and run?"

"The police don't think so. It looked like the driver deliberately targeted her."

"Okay, why does it tie into the show?" Schmidt asked.

"Because whoever did it either got incredibly lucky to see her at that moment, or he or she had a good idea when she would be leaving the Center and where she'd be going."

Schmidt looked like someone had just broken an egg over his head, surprised, horrified, and aghast. "Why would anyone hate her that much? Over a business deal gone bad? It doesn't make any sense."

"A lot of things don't seem to make sense," I answered. "Until you get all the information. Or at least enough to begin understanding what led to it."

Janice jumped back in. Anger still narrowed her blue eyes and red stained the fair complexion. "The way that detective was talking this morning, I'm pretty sure he thinks I did it. He asked me all about what I was doing Tuesday night, and could I prove it and why I hated Lorene and all that."

I drew a breath to calm myself so the words would come out evenly. "You're not alone, you know. I've talked to other people this morning who said the same thing. The way Detective Gilmont questioned them made them sure he thought they were guilty. I think that's normal for a murder investigation."

Janice huffed in a sharp breath. "He talked to her family. Those nieces?"

"You know them?" I asked.

"Met one of them once. Olive, I think her name was. Or

Olivia? Anyway, with her in charge, the company won't last more than a year or so."

And there *was a possible motive for murder, though it was hard to believe someone would go to those lengths to get rid of a competitor.*

"I see what you're thinking." The words weren't quite a sneer, but close. "Perfect reason to kill someone. And you would know. You've had a couple of murders happen here... Right?"

I gave it a moment before answering. It took a real effort to keep from shouting. "Actually, I was thinking it's a rather weak motive for murder. I'm sure it's happened, some time, some place, but I've never heard of it. Yes, we have had a couple of other murders happen here, but in both cases the victim presented a real and nasty threat to the killer." I didn't want to go too deeply into those cases. I'd had too many nightmares about them already.

"And I don't. None of us here do. So, tell that detective to quit bothering us and let us get on with our legitimate business. The same goes for you, too, Miss Assistant to the Director. Stay out of our business!" She turned and marched off, heading behind the backdrop of the booth.

"I think I'm dismissed," I muttered.

"She'll get over it."

I jumped. I'd forgotten Sam Schmidt was still there. "She gets upset easily, but it doesn't last long."

"I hope so. Thanks for understanding. I hope you're having a successful show so far?"

That question was generally a good way to get people talking, and it didn't fail this time. "Pretty good. The World Travelers Dolls are getting a great response, and Bad Boy Billy is holding his own. Our Lone Eagle series is doing unexpectedly well, though we didn't do much promo for it this time. It was the hit of the last show, and I didn't expect it to carry over as well as it has."

"Always nice to get a surprise like that. Did you get your problem with the magazine cleared up?"

He shrugged but his mouth twisted in a momentary grimace. "As well as it could be, I suppose. They'll comp us a two-page spread in the November issue. It's not as good as what we were supposed to get, but what's done is done and can't be changed. I'm settling for what I can wring from them in compensation."

I nodded. "At the risk of sounding crass or tasteless, can I ask you something? You knew Lorene Donneywell? What did you think of her?"

His expression had relaxed, but it grew tight and angry again. "I knew her. Everyone in the industry knew her. In a lot of ways. She had quite the reputation." He hesitated, looked around, and drew a deep breath. "You might as well know, since I'm sure someone here will tell you anyway... At one time Lorene and I had, well, a fling, if you will."

"An affair?"

His face flushed and a hand shook as he raised it to brush gray hair back from his forehead. "I don't think you could even characterize it as that. 'Fling' is a good word. It was brief, intense, and mostly initiated by her. She is... used to be very attractive, you know. Walking sex appeal. I certainly wasn't the only one she targeted."

Interesting verb. Always blame the woman? Or was there truth in that? "You know of others? Here?"

He shook his head slowly. "A few."

"You should tell that to Detective Gilmont. It might be worth looking into."

"I hope he won't ask me. I'd rather not say much more

about it. I definitely don't want to point a finger at anyone else."

"Even if it might help them figure out who killed Lorene?"

"There's no evidence other than my suspicion to back up what I would say. All I can say for sure is I've heard plenty of gossip and tales about how she seduced—or tried to seduce—some of the bigger players in our game. I got the impression she frequently did it very coldly, to go after information or some sort of advantage in the business."

"And you were one of them."

"Sadly, yes. It's not an episode I'm proud of. It was brief and intense before I came to my senses and realized she was using me."

I gave him my best puzzled look. "For what?"

He backed up a step and his hands twisted into fists. "I'd like to say information, but it wasn't even that. More like revenge. Someone else had just dumped her and it infuriated her. She preferred to be the one doing the dumping. She went after me as a display for the guy who parted ways with her. A part of me doesn't mind thinking I was arm candy for her, but I know better. I was someone to fill an empty space. Rather hard on the ego, but a good lesson."

"How long did it last?"

He closed his eyes for a moment. "A couple of months… every other weekend. It started during this show, five or six years ago. Before you came to work here, I think."

"I've been here for three years."

"Then it would've been before—"

A gentleman with a large case approached the booth and began checking out the displays.

Schmidt noticed him and I recognized my cue to leave.

I waved and said, "Later," as he turned and moved toward the newcomer.

I left, heading toward the thirteen hundred aisle. Scott talked to a man and woman in a booth that displayed intimidatingly complicated science sets. Only he didn't look intimidated as the woman pointed out something on one of the boxes. He looked fascinated. By the box—not the woman. The picture on the top showed a catapult, with a child adding pieces to it.

"A kid can actually build this himself?" I heard him ask.

"We tested it with a hundred or more children from ages 5 and up," the woman answered. "The younger ones needed help from adults but once they were able to read the directions, the children could do it by themselves."

"That looks like something I'd like to try."

The woman gave him a look—she was probably in her forties, but clearly not immune to an attractive man. "Stop by at the end of the show. The last day we sell everything, pretty cheaply. I'll be sure to keep one for you."

"Thanks. I'll do that." Scott straightened up and smiled at the woman. I didn't think he'd realized I was there, but he turned my way. "Everything okay?"

"Yes."

He waved goodbye to his new friends at the science kits booth, and we walked away. "Do you have a few minutes?" I asked.

He took out his phone and looked at it. "Nothing urgent here."

"Good. Walk with me. I want to show you something."

We headed toward the six hundred aisle. "The talk with Janice Langley went okay. She's still angry, and some of it's directed at me, personally, but I don't think she's going to sue or do anything outrageous. Anger seems to be part of her makeup. Or maybe it's her main motivation. Not sure how it works."

"In the same way smoothing out conflicts is part of your nature?"

I paused for a moment. "Never thought of it that way. I suppose it's true."

The smile he gave me then was different from the one he'd directed at the woman in the booth. Definitely more personal. It warmed something deep inside. I squeezed his hand to show how much I appreciated it but pushed the feelings down. Didn't need the distraction. "I talked to Sam Schmidt, too, after Janice stormed off, and that was interesting. Turns out he had a brief affair with Lorene Donneywell several years ago. According to him, a number of other men here did as well. It sounds like she tended to use and discard them, but that might be sour grapes."

Scott stopped and turned to me. "You told him to tell Gilmont?"

"I did. He doesn't want to. He doesn't want to be the one to point fingers. But I think he knew I'd relay the information. He didn't name names, though, and I don't know if he'd give them to Gilmont either. He doesn't have proof, just things he's heard, and he doesn't want to accuse anyone on that basis."

People flowed around us as Scott considered before he said, "Fair enough, I suppose. But not helpful. Tell Gilmont and let him pursue it."

"Will do." We started walking again and turned the corner into the six hundred aisle.

As we headed down the row, Scott zeroed in on the GlamourThings booth and gestured toward it. "That one. Right?"

"Right."

"What's up with it besides being ugly, gaudy, and... someone's got terrible taste in music?"

"They've got it too loud again. I've already talked to them about the music once."

"Shall I go play the heavy?" Scott's face pulled into a ferocious grimace.

"Not yet. I may have to involve you if they don't heed a second warning, though."

"Or you could do it now, and I could hang back and glower to reinforce the message."

Emilia Grinkoff stood inside the GlamourThings booth, talking with a man and a woman who both wore business suits and carried large bags. Buyers, most likely. I saw no sign of anyone else. The woman held a clipboard and was signing a paper while the man shook hands with Grinkoff. That worked for me. They were almost done, and she should be in a good humor after making a sale.

"I like the idea. Keep a close eye on the booth, though, not just us."

"Am I looking for anything in particular?"

"I'm told there's sometimes a man in the booth and he and the woman argue. The last time I came to talk to her, I'm pretty sure he was there, but hiding." I explained about seeing him peeking out. "And that's not suspicious in the least, is it?"

"Odd," Scott admitted. "But there may be reasons we don't know about."

"Like?"

"Maybe he's just shy. Or maybe—"

A strange, loud rumble and clatter rose from behind us, somewhere farther down the exhibition hall. We both turned in that direction but didn't see anything. Still the noise grew. It was both crash and rattle. Loud and getting louder. Not an explosion, exactly. Maybe more like an avalanche.

"What the hell?" Scott asked.

ELEVEN

Thursday

WITH NOTHING BUT a quick, wide-eyed glance at each other, we headed in the direction of the disturbance, joining many others with the same idea. By the time we hit the fourteen hundred aisle, it was so clogged we had to slow down and push our way through.

My phone buzzed as we got past fourteen hundred. I could barely hear Janelle above the chaos of shouts, questions, and tromping feet. "Talk loud. It's really noisy down here," I said. "Some sort of disturbance."

"That's why I'm calling," she said. "Reported situation in the sixteen hundred aisle."

"I'll say. Scott and I are trying to get there now. Will check in when I know more."

Janelle said something else I couldn't hear over the ruckus. The actual sound of whatever disaster had occurred had died down now, but I was pretty sure it had come from toward the back of the hall. Scott had the same thought. He nodded to our left, and I followed him up the aisle, picking our way through the crowd, until we got to the end. We pushed through one of the doors marked "Employees Only" and walked the dimly lit corridor running along the back of the building from the loading dock to the far end. Along the way it offered access to sets of stairs down to the lower levels as well as multiple doors back out to the exhibit hall. We used it as a shortcut to get closer to the sixteen hundred aisle without having to fight the crowd.

Once we emerged onto the show floor, the noise level assaulted my ears again.

We only reached the back end of the aisle before we had to start shoving through clots of people. Some of the bigger booths were here. The one on the left at the end spanned the seventeen hundred aisle and took up five or six spaces on each aisle. It was full of electric toys of various sorts, train sets, robots, radio-controlled cars, and other things I didn't recognize. It also held a crowd of people staring at a neighboring business. Opposite it, a line of booths featured wooden toys, magic kits, and kids' costumes.

The scene of the disaster was familiar. A crowd had gathered to gape, and I couldn't see through it. But I recognized the location and the name of the company on the banners above. PlayBlox. I'd admired some of the amazing things they had on display the previous day when I'd walked by.

By the time we pushed our way through the gathered crowd, I had some idea of what we'd find. Plastic blocks, some still bunched together, others on their own, crunched under our feet. I almost rolled my ankle when my foot slipped on a blue plastic piece three inches long and an inch high.

Still, I gasped when I finally got a look at the destruction. My heart did one of those stutter-step-then-clench numbers, and my stomach twisted into a knot. I muttered a few curse words under my breath.

The life-size Abraham Lincoln I'd admired the previous day had been toppled on its side with a long crack diagonally through the figure where a series of blocks had separated. His hat, one hand, and part of his beard had come loose, the beard devolved into clumps of brown blocks. The Washington monument must have been better braced. It still stood, though a smattering of white blocks on the floor around it came from several craters in the structure's surface.

Pieces had come loose from the spaceship as well, leaving a cracked body on the table. The fairy castle suffered the worst damage. Most of its towers had been dislodged and either crumbled or hung by a block or two from the walls they clung to. Its gate and some crenellations were completely smashed.

All that work and loving care destroyed in minutes. I struggled to hold back tears.

One of the bins holding blocks put out for people to experiment with had been knocked on its side, spreading even more small obstacles around the area.

Beside me, Scott muttered, "What the hell happened here?"

Nearby someone said, "Drone." A couple of others echoed the word. I looked at one of them. "Did you say drone?"

"I did. I saw it," the woman replied. "Couldn't tell you anything more than it was big and dark blue, but I heard a crash and looked over in time to see it smack into the castle. Then it went for the spaceship. It had already knocked over the Lincoln figure and tried to do the same to the Washington Monument. It looked like someone was deliberately steering it right into things."

"Is it still around?"

"Flew off. Hit that spaceship, rose almost to the ceiling and headed off."

"Which way?"

The woman thought. "It circled for a minute and went

that way." She pointed toward the southwest corner of the building and the lower numbered rows. "I didn't see exactly where it went, though."

I thanked her and scanned the area. Scott was talking to a man in the far corner of the booth who must work there; he looked devastated, shoulders slumped and expression glum.

I joined them in time to hear him say, "...came out of nowhere. I didn't even see it until it smashed into Old Abe there." He glanced at the president's statue, and I caught the shine of tears in his eyes. "I hope he can be put back together. Oh my God."

He stared out over the sea of brightly colored blocks. Generous and compassionate souls had started gathering them, and some took care to preserve larger chunks where the pieces hadn't all come apart. Aside from the helpers, the rest of the crowd began to dissipate, though for a while those who'd been in back took the opportunity to get a closer look.

I wanted to support the people at the booth, but Scott and others seemed to be doing a good job of it. I had another mission, and I had to pursue it while memories were fresh. But first...

I glanced behind me to see Craig Vincelli arriving on the scene. I grabbed him and said, "Relay to everyone at the doors...if anyone tries to leave with a drone or any large boxes or packages, they should stop them and notify us right away."

I'm not sure how coherent it was, but Craig got the picture. We've worked together long enough that he asked no questions but got right on his phone to put the word out. He started toward Scott once he'd finished.

"I'm going to try to chase down the drone," I told him.

Craig frowned. "No tackling anyone on your own. You find it, you let us know."

"I will."

Since the woman had suggested the drone had moved in a southwesterly direction, I pushed through the crowd, heading toward the front, but turned right when I got to the center aisle, passed the fifteen hundred aisle and swung into the fourteen hundreds. Handley Vehicles, the booth where the electric cars had been vandalized, stood at the far end, but I only went up past a couple of booths. At the largest of the three on my left, I approached a pair of people manning the display and identified myself as Center Personnel and asked, "Did any of you see a drone fly past here a few minutes ago?"

"I did," a young woman said. From the next booth a man who had overheard the question added, "So did I."

"Which way did it go?"

"It dipped a couple of times," the woman said, "then it headed that way." Again, she pointed to the southwest. The man nodded agreement. I called, "Thanks," as I turned and went to the center aisle again. I skipped a couple more aisles and stopped at a corner booth at twelve hundred. No one at the first booth I asked at remembered seeing a drone, but at the one opposite, an older man said, "Yup. Saw it zoom right over. I heard it buzzing, and it zipped over the corner there."

"Which way did it go?" I asked again.

And again, he pointed to the southwest. Back to the center aisle I went and past Carrie Classics at the end of the eleven hundred aisle. I turned left, away from it, toward the front. Three booths down I found someone who'd seen the drone go by. It sounded as if it had climbed higher at that point but was still heading southwest. So I continued, stopping twice more and asking around until I found someone who'd seen it. The second time I had to inquire at several booths before getting an answer.

I'd moved so far toward the entrances by then, I used the front aisle, rushing past the main sets of doors. At three hundred, I found two people who'd seen it. Both said it appeared to be coming down, angling toward the far corner near where the west and south walls met.

I heard raised voices coming from that direction and saw people gathering as I approached the corner. Sure enough, a large blue drone lay on the floor in their midst. It must've been at least five feet by four feet, with rotors rising a foot or more above the center main part of the body. A quick glance around didn't reveal anyone obviously operating the thing, though several people had pulled out cell phones and were taking pictures.

When a man reached down toward it, I ran up and said, "Don't touch it. It may be evidence in a crime." I identified myself as Center personnel and asked everyone to take a step back, then called for Security. While we waited, I asked the group, "Did anyone see the operator?"

People looked around at each other and the area, but all bore surprised, baffled expressions. Several shook their heads in the negative.

One man said, "They can be operated from some distance away. This one has a camera so probably the pilot was using that to guide it. He could be anywhere. On the other side of the room, even." Others nodded agreement.

I spotted Craig approaching and asked everyone to step back for him. I gave him a quick summary of what I knew—not much—and watched him put on latex gloves before lifting the drone. It had the manufacturer's name on the bottom, and I recognized it as being a current exhibitor.

Craig also asked the group if anyone had seen the drone

land, and a few said they had. They mostly agreed that it just sailed down out of the air, plunked itself on the floor, and stayed there. No one had noticed anyone who looked like they might be directing it.

Craig picked it up by one corner, and we walked back toward the booth where it had done its destructive work. Several curious onlookers followed us.

"Do we call the police about this?" I asked him.

"Not a simple yes or no," Craig answered. "Not sure what the exhibitor wants. Probably Janelle needs to decide."

We got back to the booth to find Scott still huddled with a man and two women there. Abe had been set upright again, hat and hand restored, his beard not so neat as it had been. Craters remained in the Washington Monument, but the scattered debris was removed. A young man and woman worked on putting the spaceship back together, while the castle awaited further attention. Anger flashed through me as I stared at those remains and remembered what they had been before. What sort of lowlife would do something so malicious?

Everyone looked up as we approached, and eyes widened at the sight of the drone. The older man in the group stood, expression tight, body vibrating with tension. He reached out for it, but Craig snatched it back, away from his grasp.

The man let out a hissing breath. "I want to smash that thing into a million pieces!"

"Understood." Scott put a hand on his arm. "But it's evidence and it might lead us to the person who was guiding it."

My phone buzzed. I moved away from the group to answer since it was from the front desk.

"Hey, Heather, this is Callie at the front desk. You wanted to know when Kevin Donneywell arrived so you could approve his badge."

"Oh. Right. I can't get there right now but check his ID and put my initials in as approving it."

"Will do."

I'd need to look in on the Donneywells again, but it would wait until later.

Craig and Scott had the situation with the destroyed block sculptures as well in hand as possible when I got back. And it appeared the disaster had a positive side for the exhibitor. Though the man in charge still huddled with the security people, four younger sales associates were all now engaged with potential customers. Many of those likely came to view the results of the calamity, but they stayed to listen to the sales pitches. I hoped some would submit orders.

Another group of buyers approached and the man in charge nodded as Craig and Scott finished. As we left, he went to greet the newcomers.

"Looks like they got one small silver lining," I said, as much to make myself feel better about the situation as anything else. "Still… We've got to find out who's behind this."

Walking toward the doors to head upstairs, I noted that people were starting to close their booths for the evening. A glance at my watch showed it was twenty to six.

"We're heading up to talk to Janelle about this," Scott told me.

"I'm with you." We got into the private elevator and got off on the office level.

Janelle waited for us in her office. "Did I hear right? Someone drove a drone into some of the PlayBlox displays?" She stared at the machine Craig held at his side. "Is that the culprit?"

"Heather chased it down." He set it on her desk. "Don't touch it, please. We may want to get it checked for fingerprints."

Janelle pulled her hand back. "Tell me what you know."

Scott related how we'd heard the crash, went to investigate, and found the destruction. While I went off to chase it down, he talked to the people in the booth. They thought hard but couldn't come up with anyone who would have a motive for the destruction. As far as any of them knew, they had no enemies. Possibly some jealous rivals, but none with feelings strong enough to motivate that kind of attack. They hadn't received any threats prior to it. No disenchanted employees. They were willing to co-operate with a police investigation. In fact, they demanded it.

Janelle said, "I'll make the call. They'll want to talk to you. I think it can wait until morning, though."

Scott nodded agreement. "I also asked everyone still in the area about the drone. A couple of people noticed it right before it smashed into the block statues, but I couldn't find anyone who saw where it came from. Heather went after where it landed."

Janelle looked at me. "You chased the drone?"

"I followed the path of people who'd seen it until I got to where it came down. It was sitting on the floor, but there didn't seem to be anyone around steering it. Someone mentioned it has a camera so it could be operated remotely."

"From anywhere inside the building?"

"Maybe even outside," Scott said. "I have no idea what range the controllers on these things have."

"But we do know the manufacturer, and they have a booth here."

Scott said, "I doubt anyone from the company would be stupid enough to use one of their own drones this way, but they can tell us if one has been stolen. At the least they can give us some idea of the range of the controller. Maybe even a way to trace it?"

"We're not likely to be that lucky," Janelle said. "But the more we know the better."

"I'll talk to them first thing in the morning," Scott offered.

"Can I tag along?"

"Can I say no?"

"Absolutely not," I answered.

"There you go then." He mock-sighed and looked at the bright blue machine on Janelle's desk. "Can you get pictures of it to show the people at the booth? Get the model number?"

"Sure." I pulled out my phone. For the next few minutes Craig lifted and turned the drone various ways so I could get pictures from different angles. I reviewed them and said, "I think that should do it. I hope they can give us a clue."

"I do, too," Scott said. "I wonder. Could this be related to the vandalism at Hanley? There's no obvious connection other than the sheer apparent randomness of it. But they do have that in common. No clear motivation for either one."

Craig shrugged. "There's a lot we don't know yet."

TWELVE

Friday

I GOT TO the office before everyone else the next morning. I'd spent nearly every moment of the last couple of days on the show floor. My inbox had papers flowing over the sides, and the email list clocked in at one hundred and twenty-two unread messages.

The contents of each of the inboxes had shrunk by the time I heard the elevator ping and the sound of voices emerging from it. Janelle and Scott came in together, and I relegated the rest of the paperwork to "handle later" status. I already had a list of things I needed to do that day; visiting the drone company was at the top.

Janelle reminded me Dennis Michaelton was coming back to work today. All else being quiet, she planned a little welcome back celebration in the shipping department around one thirty. We didn't call it a party since we were in the middle of a show. Just a drop-in to say hello. She hoped we'd all join her there.

I had a couple of minor things to sort out with Janelle while Scott checked in with Craig in the security office, then we headed down to the show floor.

Tinstall Machines had the last six spaces between the twenty-two hundred and twenty-three hundred aisles. Pedestals of varying heights lined either side of the booth, each holding a drone. They came in a surprising variety of sizes, shapes, weights, and colors. Toward the center back a larger table held a multi-level display of boxes of various sized machines with a sign announcing a huge giveaway for attendees who signed up.

In front of it, a young sales rep demonstrated flying a small drone. It was only about ten inches square, but its four propellers lifted it maybe twenty feet off the floor. The man guided it in circles, did figure-eights, had it dip and swirl around people, and even turned it over in mid-air and made it fly upside down. Scott and I both watched in fascination for a couple of minutes before we drew back and looked around for someone who appeared to be in charge. The sales associates all wore bright blue polo shirts with the company logo over their pockets, so I snagged one and asked. He pointed to a woman near the back corner, consulting with another of the associates about something on an order sheet. We waited for them to finish before approaching.

Allison Fortunato, according to her exhibitor badge, had straight blond hair showing a few streaks of gray. The smile she gave us seemed genuine and didn't fade even when she noted our Center Personnel IDs. She shook hands with each of us as we introduced ourselves. "What can I do for you?"

I let Scott take the lead. He could do charming when needed, and I thought this might be one of those times.

"We need your help," he said. "If you were around yesterday afternoon, you probably heard the crash over at the PlayBlox Toys booth."

"I heard it. A couple of our guys went over to check out what had happened and said a bunch of figures were smashed. They said it was a drone—" She looked from me

Scott to me and back, noting our expressions. "Oh man. One of ours?"

"I'm afraid so." Seeing her stiffen, he rushed to add, "We don't think any of your people did this, but we hope you can help us identify the drone and let us know if anyone borrowed one, or if you gave one away to someone here."

She sighed heavily. "I don't think it could've been one of my people. They were all here in the booth at the time. We've had good crowds and we've needed all hands on deck." She grinned briefly. "A good problem to have, right?"

We both agreed. I pulled out my phone and brought up the pictures. "This is what it looked like."

She took the phone from me. "Oh, that's interesting. It's a P-620."

"What's particularly interesting about it?" Scott asked.

She handed the phone back. "It's one of our top-of-the-line models. We were supposed to have two here at the show to demo, but one of them went missing early on. At first, we thought it hadn't arrived at all, that our shipping department made a mistake, but when I asked, they swore they had packed two. It had been double-checked. But they were put in a crate with a couple of other models and when we started unloading, we only found one. Tom was upset about it. He's our best pilot and would have been the one doing the demo with it."

"You noticed it was missing on set-up day?"

She nodded. "We planned for two. One was to be used for demos and one would be part of our mega-giveaway. In fact, it was supposed to be the cherry at the top of the display. We had to make do when we couldn't find it."

"You asked your people about it and if they'd seen anyone messing around with the box it should've come in?"

"Of course. Kris opened the box and began pulling things out, but we had a problem with the backdrop, and she went to help sort that out. When she came back, it wasn't there. She was only away for ten minutes or so and the box should've been in sight the whole time. But the backdrop was being a pill, and I expect there were times no one was watching the merchandise."

"Is it possible this isn't the missing drone? That this is one someone bought somewhere and brought in?"

Allison thought about it. "Possible but not too likely. It's one of our newest models so it hasn't been on sale long."

Scott looked at the young man doing the demo. "How hard is it to control these things? Would it have to be done by someone who knew it well?"

Allison clearly didn't like where that was going, and I didn't blame her. But I think she tried to be honest about the situation. "It takes some practice to pilot a drone. And if this one was used to crash a bunch of PlayBlox sculptures, it would suggest someone who had some practice, who was fairly skilled in it. But that wouldn't mean they had to know this model specifically. Controls aren't much different from other models on the market."

"Do all of the people from your company here know how to fly it?"

She tapped her fingers on the display shelf as she considered. "I don't think so. We all know enough about them to explain how they work. But for demos, Tom's our go-to guy. If he's not available, Kris can do it. They both have the apps on their phones."

Scott focused on the last sentence. "You need an app on your phone?"

"Not necessarily. You can fly them with a remote. This is where it gets complicated, depending on the model, because some remotes, like this one, give you a lot more flight information than others. For some, you need visual contact to fly without a smartphone app. The remote on this can give enough telemetry to guide it, if you know what you're looking at. But if you're using a camera on the drone, you need the app for visual. And for guidance if it's out of sight or you're not used to the flight data display. Given their range, most people will use the phone app along with the controls."

I could almost see the implications of that info percolating through Scott's brain. As they were doing in my mind, too.

"Would the phone keep track of past flights?" Scott asked.

"Depends on the app. Most do, although I think it's one of those things you can toggle on and off."

Scott's expression changed to what I thought of as his "reassuring mode". "I doubt any of your employees was responsible for this, but I will need to talk to each of them, especially the two who do demo flights. It's mostly about eliminating them as suspects."

"Are you with the police?" she asked.

"No. I'm Market Center Security. So, no, I have no authority to compel anyone to talk to me."

"I've already told you everyone was in the booth at the time the drone smashed those things. We were having a very busy time and I needed everyone working."

"I understand. Mostly I want to get a better understanding of how the things work. Also, I'm hoping one of your people would be able to point me to someone else here who might know about piloting a drone. Maybe they've even talked to someone and given them pointers."

Allison looked both relieved and dubious. "We've given

lots of people pointers, but if you think it might help track down who did this, we'll make it happen."

"I do. The sooner, the better," Scott said. "Can I talk to the people who are here now?"

"As long as we don't get too busy and need them selling."

"Understood, of course."

My phone buzzed and Janelle's name showed on the caller ID. I excused myself and walked a few steps away to take the call.

"Not desperately urgent," Janelle said, "But I'm getting reports of a man sneaking around the four to six hundred aisles. Reports are he creeps behind curtains and back-drops and hides when anyone official comes around the area. He hasn't done anything bad as far as I can tell, but it's got some of the people on the aisle uncomfortable and wondering what's going on. Can you check it out when you get a minute?" She gave me the names of a couple of people who'd complained.

"Will do. I recognize the aisle number and suspect I know who they're talking about. I'll report back in a bit."

I told Scott I needed to follow up on some other issues. He could handle the questioning better than I could, and there was no need for both of us to be tied up with it. He promised to fill me in later.

I headed for the six hundred aisle, trying to decide how to go about finding out who the man was and why he was hiding in the shadows. I needed to learn as much as I could before I tackled Emilia Grinkoff directly, so I aimed for the booth where I'd first learned of the elusive man's existence.

"Oh, yeah, we've seen him again," the older gentleman in charge at the booth told me. "He goes in and out, but seems kind of... I don't know. Furtive?"

"Does he have a badge?"

"He has a badge, but I haven't gotten a good look at it."

"When was the last time you saw him?"

"Yesterday. Near closing time. He went into the booth from the back, cutting through one of the spaces behind."

I handed him one of my cards. "I have some others to talk to before I tackle this head on over there, but can I ask you to give me a call as soon as possible, next time you see him?"

"Sure. Will do."

I thanked him and went to talk to the other two people Janelle had suggested. One of them was with a customer, so I moved on and found the other, who proved to be an ebullient young woman with big hair, big frame, and a big laugh. When I introduced myself and told her why I was there, her face grew abruptly serious. "Yeah, he's creeping me out," she said. "Cutting through the booth like he owns it or going around the back to the other side. He shuffles and mutters and he never responds when you try to hail him. Ignores you completely."

I asked her to describe him and got the same general idea the man in the booth across the aisle from GlamourThings had given: tall, heavy-set, somewhere between forty and fifty, dark hair laced with gray, mustache, and a heavy, fleshy face. The woman tended to talk with her hands, waving them all over, randomly. I tried not to be distracted by her gestures.

"Does he have a show badge?"

She had to think about it for a moment. Her hands paused, then her fingers twirled figure eights in the air. "Good question. Yeah, I think he does. At least, he's got something on a cord around his neck. I haven't looked at it too closely."

"How often have you seen him?" I asked.

"Probably half a dozen times. He comes and goes. He

doesn't act like he has any real purpose here. I get the idea he's just wandering around. Either that or—" Her face broke into a more ironic grin. "Maybe he's some kind super industrial spy and the walking around is a cover for checking things out."

She laughed at my dubious raised eyebrow.

"Yeah, okay, I don't buy it either," she admitted. "I don't understand what he's doing here, though."

"Do you feel threatened by him?" I asked.

"That's a good question." Her hands went up and waved again. "I guess not exactly threatened. More puzzled. Maybe a little concerned he'll put off potential customers."

"Valid concern." I thanked her for the information and moved on to the next person. The man at a booth two spaces up gave the same basic description. "He wanders through our booth like he owns it," the man complained. "Ignores people when they ask him to stay away. And he almost tore down part of the backdrop pushing through to the other side. I don't know what he's doing or why, but I don't want him blundering around our booth. It's not good for business."

I agreed and admitted I understood his concerns. I assured him we were on top of it and would have a talk with him and the people at the company who'd provided the badge.

After that I took a short walk around the floor, trying to decide how to handle this. We've had gatecrashers before, and there's a standard protocol for those situations, but it didn't apply if he had a valid show badge.

Mentally braced for another confrontation with Emilia Grinkoff, I returned to the booth, and found it tended by a girl I'd never seen before. She couldn't have been more than twenty, but she pinned on a professional smile and approached me. "Fashion dolls are having a resurgence with today's girls," she said, launching into her sales pitch.

I introduced myself, explained my function, and asked about Emilia. "Oh," the girl paused and stared at me for a moment as if deciding what she ought to say. She settled for the generic, "She's taking a break. She should be back in fifteen minutes or so. Do you want me to give her a message?"

"No. That's all right. I'll catch up with her later." I looked around but didn't see anyone else. I tried the usual gambit for getting people to talk. "How's business?"

It fell flat this time. "Sorry, I'm a fill-in here. I don't know."

"Do you help out here often?"

She shook her head. "I'm a temp. Mostly working in the Metrall booth down there." She pointed toward the next aisle over and few booths up. "Ms. Grinkoff asked if she could borrow me to keep a watch on the booth while she went to get something to eat. My boss said it was okay. So here I am. I just read through the pitch a few minutes ago."

I looked around. "Is there anyone else helping in the booth?"

"Other than Ms. Grinkoff? Not as far as I know."

"Oh. Okay." I sighed and checked my phone as I left. I had time to visit the Donneywell booth before lunch and no other messages at the moment.

On the way there, I was stopped several times by people who recognized me. Some wanted to know if the rumors about Lorene Donneywell's murder were true. Others inquired about the drone attack the previous day and if we'd caught the perpetrator.

I walked a fine line answering those questions. If I said we knew nothing, it would sound like the Center wasn't taking the problems seriously. But if I admitted how little we actually knew, it would likely scare people. I tried for the middle ground. I told them the police were investigating; the Center was doing all we could to cooperate; and we felt confident the authorities were on top of it all.

I less than half-believed it myself, but I must've been reasonably convincing since most people seemed satisfied. Maybe I was a better actress than I realized. Or being around salespeople all day every day let the techniques rub off on me.

A rush of laughter and applause sidetracked me, and I went to find the cause. The sound drew me to a familiar area. A growing group of people surrounded the Carrie Classics booth, fascinated by a performance going on.

I had to maneuver through the crowd to reach a spot where I could see the show. Tables and racks had been moved to the edges of the booth to leave an open space in the middle. Sam Schmidt and Ross Langley stood near the back, watching as three figures dressed in cowboy outfits pantomimed what appeared to be the aftermath of a robbery. Two of the actors wore all black, from boots to hats, marking them as the villains, I supposed. Off to one side, Janice Langley flaunted a long silk dress in a fashion popular in the late nineteenth century. From her feigned tears and exaggerated handwringing, I deduced she played the part of the robbery victim.

The third cowboy actor wore beige trousers, a white shirt with a leather vest, and a white hat atop a false head modeled on the "Bad Boy Billy" figures. I still couldn't figure out what kind of animal he was supposed to be. The snout reminded me of a horse but the eyes at the top looked straight ahead instead of being on the sides. His gloves suggested a cross between human hand and hoof, but the fingers were flexible enough for him to wield a large staff with ease as he chased after the villains. The latter ran in circles around the booth and hid behind strategically placed shelves and tables.

The three male actors were clearly trained in comedy play-acting and pulling off pratfalls. The chase went on far longer than it should have with all three tripping over thin air, overlooking obvious hiding spots, and missing clear opportunities for capture. But the performers made it hilarious, and I laughed along with the others gathered there and clapped when the playlet concluded with Bad Boy Billy overcoming the villains and then marching them off to "jail" behind the booth's backdrop.

I moved toward Janice to tell her what a nice job they'd done with that bit of theater, but too many people were intrigued by the product and crowded into the booth, quickly occupying all of the staff. I backed off.

The little play lifted my spirits and improved my mood, reminding me why the Toy Show was usually so much fun.

After wandering and basking in good feelings for a few minutes, I made my way to the Donneywell booth. I said hello to the giant dragon, who was starting to feel like an old friend. A glance at the people present there explained the transformation in Jessie's demeanor and grooming.

THIRTEEN

Friday

THE YOUNG MAN in the booth with Jessie and the Donney-wells could explain a whole roomful of makeovers. Mid-twenties, with dark hair, chiseled features, and a lean, athletic build, he radiated charm and charisma.

Only one customer was in the booth, attended by Olivia, and the rest of them turned to me as I walked up.

Angelina looked pleased to see me, Jessie seemed wary, and the young man turned on a megawatt smile. "You must be Kevin," I said, holding out a hand as I introduced myself.

He took my hand and smiled. "Thank you for t-t-taking care of getting my badge ready," he said.

"No problem. I'm sorry you had to come here under such sad circumstances."

The smile dimmed and took a turn for the wry. "Me, too." Color rose in his cheeks. "I mean, I'm… I'm not s-s-sorry to be here." He looked over at his aunts and Jessie. "In fact… But the circumstances… It's hard to b-b-believe Aunt Lorene is gone. I keep waiting for her to show up and tell us it was all a b…b…a joke."

So good looks had some limitations. He had a speech impediment.

His expression grew even more serious. "I c-c-can't fold

my mind around it. That anyone so vibrant, so…alive, can
stop being, just that quickly. It really makes you think about
things."

"True," I agreed. "None of us know how much time
we have."

He nodded. "We n-n-need to make the time we have
count."

Angelina and Jessie closed in on us. "Has that nosy detective gotten anywhere in investigating Lorene's death?"
Angelina asked. "It's been more than a day now."

"I don't know. The police don't share much with us."

"They have…have to look at us closely," Kevin said.
"Statistics say most murders are committed by people the
victim knew. And we…we're the only ones who stand to
b-b-benefit from it."

"I'm not so sure of that." Jessie spoke for the first time.
We all looked at her. "No, I don't know anything or anyone
specific. But I suspect she knew things about people here,
some things they might not want others to know."

"You told Detective Gilmont about those?" I asked.

She rolled her eyes. "I told him what I just told you. But
when I couldn't give him anything more specific, he kind
of pooh-poohed it."

And once again I had the impression she wanted someone to push her to reveal more about what she suspected,
but she wasn't going to do it here, in front of the others. I
had to figure out how to get her away and squeeze her for
information.

Olivia finished with the customer and joined us, but
asked Jessie, "Has Dougal been nominated for the Plaything of the Year Awards?"

"Of course. I think he's a shoo-in for the License and
Plush categories."

"Good." Olivia smiled at her son, then turned to me. "Did they ask you what the police have learned about Lorene's death?"

"They did." I reiterated what I'd told the others. A group of five or six buyers approached the booth and I took that as my cue to leave. I texted Scott to tell him I was heading for lunch.

Shortly after I'd sat down with my slice of pizza, he joined me, carrying a hamburger and soft drink. "I hope your morning's been better than mine," he said as he snagged a chair with a foot and yanked it out.

"Some," I said. I told him about the theatrics I'd seen at Carrie Classics. He smiled at my recounting of the little play, though I realized that kind of comedy had to be seen to be appreciated. Mostly it sounded silly in the retelling. "And we haven't had any more disasters." I stopped and took a breath. "Maybe I shouldn't say so. The day's still got a few hours to go. What made yours such a bear?"

"Apparently some local group of teenagers heard about the show and decided it would be a great adventure to see if they could crash it."

"Any of them make it through?"

"Three we know of. Took us almost an hour to round them up."

"Argh. Not fun. What did you do about them?"

"Put on my best terrifying cop face, warned them if it happened again, we'd take them downtown and book them for trespassing, and sent them on their way."

I studied his now not-at-all-terrifying face and saw the glint in his eyes. "You had them quaking in their tennies, I'll bet."

"Yup. I think they got the message."

"And you didn't give yourself away even the least little bit?"

"What? Give what away?"

"How many times did you do something like that when you were a kid?" I asked.

The glint sharpened. "I can honestly say I never tried to sneak into a trade show."

"What did you sneak into? Don't tell me you never did. I don't believe it."

"Think you know me so well?" His mouth quirked into a half-grin. "True, I did get into a movie theater a couple of times by a side door. Once a group of us even tried to crash a Sixers game."

"Sixers... That's Philly's pro basketball team? Bold! Did you get caught?"

"At the Sixers game. Yes."

"What happened?"

"They called our parents to come get us. My dad told me how much I'd disappointed him, and he'd thought I was more mature and trustworthy than that. Made me feel like the lowest sort of lifeform. Then I was grounded for six weeks and had to help clean out the attic."

"Bet it taught you a lesson."

His smile turned thoughtful. "The worst thing was my parents' disappointment. I didn't like being grounded and the attic was hot and dusty, but those didn't make me feel as bad knowing I'd broken their trust."

"Good lesson to remember about parenting." And because that could easily go in a direction I wasn't ready to talk about, I decided to change the subject. "What about talking to the drone people? Did you get anything useful?"

Scott's quirked brow acknowledged what I was doing and why. "Not much more than we learned yesterday. It doesn't sound like it was one of their people piloting the drone. Everyone independently verified one went missing on the first day. And they all have good alibis for the time frame."

"Why doesn't that surprise me?" I sighed.

"I got Craig's approval to hire someone to review video for us. For the first day when it was likely stolen and for the actual attack. We know what time the drone struck, but even so, there's a lot to go over since the pilot could've been anywhere, even outside the exhibit hall."

"I wonder…?"

It seemed too far-fetched even to mention, but Scott prompted when I paused. "What?"

"Two thoughts, actually. First, is this related to the vandalism of the car at Handley?"

"Good question." He took a moment to bite into the hamburger, chew, and swallow. "In lieu of any other explanation for either incident, I'm leaning toward yes."

"I am, too. It almost seems like someone's trying to send a message."

"To everyone here, or specific people?"

"If we knew that we'd have a better handle on who and why."

"True, and—"

"May I join you?" I looked up to see Janelle holding a box from the Chinese food stand.

"Of course," I said.

"Sorry if I'm interrupting something personal, but there are things we need to talk about."

"Personal conversation ended about ten minutes ago," Scott said, grinning.

I frowned at him, which drew a short laugh from Janelle. "We were discussing the vandalism incidents and wondering if they're related," I told her. "Maybe there's some kind of pattern we can't see yet."

"Fill me in. Did you get any leads on the drone?"

Scott repeated what he'd told me earlier. I updated her on what I'd learned about the man roaming the six hundred aisle and what was going on at the Donneywell booth.

"Does Detective Gilmont have any good leads to Lorene Donneywell's murder?" I asked once I'd finished the update.

Janelle unwrapped two eggrolls and took a bite of one, chewing before she answered, "Not as far as I know. He's made several of our exhibitors quite unhappy with his questions."

"I've been hearing about it."

"Necessary evil, I'm afraid," Janelle said. "I've got another one for you."

My stomach clenched and I set down the pizza crust I was getting ready to chew on. "What?"

"I need you to go to the Awards Gala tomorrow night. Both of you." She glanced from me to Scott.

"I figured I'd probably end up going, but what's up?"

"The National Playthings Association got a threatening message. They've turned the actual written note over to the police. I can't remember the exact wording, but it was vague, something like, 'Your awards night could be a real bore. Or maybe it will be more exciting than you want!'"

I glanced at Scott, who looked puzzled.

"If that's a threat, it couldn't get much vaguer," I said.

"No one's panicking, but we do need to take it seriously," Janelle said.

Scott nodded agreement. "Given what's been going on here, I think it needs to be taken very seriously."

FOURTEEN

"THAT'S WHY I want all hands on deck for the dinner," Janelle said. "I've talked to Craig and we're requesting extra security for the event, but since it's being held across the street, there's only so much we can do. I passed it on to Gilmont, too."

Big fancy gala parties normally happened in connection with major shows or conferences. We could accommodate some in the ballrooms downstairs, but most took place at the hotel across the street, which had facilities for more glamorous banquets and high-class events. We cooperated with them as much as possible, but we weren't in charge of those.

"I'm guessing this isn't for public consumption yet?" I asked.

"No. I'm meeting with the Association leaders and awards committee later today to discuss what to say. If there's a real threat, it's not fair to keep people in the dark. On the other hand, we don't want to cause a panic if there's really nothing to it."

I frowned. "Don't envy you having to make that decision."

"It's not mine to make, thank goodness. I can only advise the committee."

"Which may be even harder."

"I won't say it isn't." She put her napkin in the empty box and replaced the cover. "Time to head down to the shipping department to welcome Dennis back to work."

Scott and I had both finished, so we gathered our trash and stood with her. After dumping the containers in the bins, the three of us headed to the show floor, going across it along one side to stay clear of the main area and reaching the shipping department.

This area wasn't one of my favorite places to be, ever since I'd found a body in a trash bin just outside the loading docks a few months ago. I tried to put that out of my mind, though, and be welcoming. Dennis Michaelton had been out for almost six months, getting chemotherapy, and he'd missed a lot of time even before then. Andrea and other staff members had come down from the office with trays of cookies and pitchers of punch to welcome him back.

We surprised Dennis in the midst of going through a box full of paperwork that had been piling up since he'd left last January. He seemed genuinely touched we'd made this effort for him.

After a bit of mingling, Scott introduced himself to Dennis and engaged him in conversation, asking him about his illness and treatments. Thirty minutes into the gathering, my phone buzzed with a text message telling me the elusive wanderer was back in the GlamourThings booth. I held up the phone to indicate to Janelle I had something I needed to do and scooted back to the show floor.

I made my way to the six hundred aisle but didn't go directly to the target. If possible, I wanted to catch the man in or near the GlamourThings booth. I stopped a couple of places away on the other side and tried to stay in the shadow of a group of buyers lined up to play a promotional Bingo game in a space that featured boxes of toy soldiers. I craned my neck to see across into the GlamourThings booth. Unfortunately, the only person there was Emilia Grinkoff, showing a series of doll accessories to two men in suits. I looked around but found no sign of someone matching the description.

Five minutes later, I gave up and went to the man who'd texted me. He looked chagrined as I approached. "I'm sorry. He walked away a few minutes ago. I tried to get a picture of him, but he disappeared before I got the app open."

My annoyance flared. The guy was hard to pin down. "Did you see if he had an Exhibitor's badge?" I asked.

"He has one and I think it's legit. Couldn't read the name on it."

I thanked him. Then I strolled up the six hundred aisle, went left at the center break and down five hundred, keeping my eyes open. Once I thought I saw a big man duck behind a backdrop, but when I got to the vicinity I couldn't find anyone except a young woman restocking a display shelf.

I stopped and asked, "Did you see a man come this way? A rather large man, middle-aged, with dark, rumpled hair? I thought I saw him, but he disappeared."

She blinked twice, gave me a blank look, and shook her head. "No. Sorry."

I had my doubts. I felt pretty sure I'd seen the man nearby. I looked around but didn't see anyone else in the booth. Two people in the next one showed off big ploofy stuffed animals to a couple of buyers and paid no attention to anything else.

I gave up and turned away. Walking around for a few minutes yielded no further sight of the man. I returned to the GlamourThings booth and caught Emilia Grinkoff waiting with no customers. Her eyes narrowed, though her lips formed a smile as she saw me approach. Tinkly music came from a speaker at the back, but the volume was reasonable.

"You have word on changing our booth?" she asked.

"No, I'm afraid not. As I've already told you, we don't have any place for you to move to. The show is entirely full, and we can't ask anyone else to relocate." Before she could respond, I added, "We've had some complaints about things happening in your booth. People are concerned about the noise. Loud voices and arguments as well as the loud music."

I didn't see any evidence of someone hiding behind the curtains. "We've also had complaints about a man who seems to be associated with this booth cutting through other exhibitors' spaces. He's bothering people."

She gave me a blank look, surprisingly similar to the one I'd gotten from the girl earlier. "I don't know what you're talking about." Her words were equally unconvincing.

I watched her steadily. She knew, all right. But she was holding the course and at the moment I had no leverage. She knew that, too. I conceded defeat. "All right. But the noise has to be controlled. You can't play music or argue so loudly it interferes with other conversations around here." We'd been through this before, of course.

Grinkoff kept a straight face and said, "I'm keeping the music lower. They're jealous of how many customers we have."

"Perhaps they are, but that doesn't change anything. You need to be careful not to interfere with your neighbors' business."

I left it at that and walked away. Swallowing my frustration, I surveyed the aisle. Commerce carried on around me.

So, what next? I could go back to the shipping area

where the gathering was probably winding down, but I felt too restless and anxious.

I considered what others had said about the tension hanging over the show. Something definitely swirled in the air. Trade shows were always frantic and over-the-top, of course. Too many people had too much at stake for it to be anything else. But good business practice dictated that the exhibitors keep things light and fun and have everyone maintain their sense of humor as much as possible. Optimism was always the order of the day. Smart companies sent only their best salespeople to a trade show. An almost carnival-like atmosphere usually prevailed.

I stopped again and looked around. Buyers bustled by, tromping from one booth to the next collecting brochures and samples. In nearby spaces sales associates made their pitches. Some handed out pens and candy to attract attention. The pens were a disappointing array of standard, cheap ballpoints. I loved great pens, and collected the more interesting ones, but so far I hadn't seen any exciting versions here.

Other displays had big bowls where people could drop their business cards or fill out a form to be enrolled in raffles. Off to my left a group laughed at the antics of a wind-up toy duck that waddled around one buyer, quacking. Slightly farther down the aisle, a crowd gathered around a table featuring boxes where people could actually play with some kind of doughy substance which both sparkled and stretched but left no residue on hands or clothing.

I hoped most people had no idea anything different or threatening was going on. That was how it was supposed to be. Part of my job involved making sure they remained blissfully ignorant and commerce ran smoothly.

But knowing the way the rumor mill ran rampant at

these events, most of them likely had some idea of a vague threat over the show. They would surely have heard of Lorene Donneywell's murder and the vandalism at some of the booths. Probably most would tell themselves it had nothing to do with them. I hoped that would prove true.

I stopped near the Carrie Classics booth. Janice Langley was there by herself for the moment with no customers. She'd changed from the elaborate period dress of earlier into a standard business suit. Traffic seemed quiet. A prominent and popular marketing guru had a presentation scheduled for today so maybe that explained the empty area. The opportunity was too good to let pass, no matter how reluctant I was to tackle the lioness.

She watched me approach with no obvious expression and spoke before I could even open my mouth. "Have the cops figured out who killed Lorene?"

"Not as far as I know."

"So, you're still being their eyes and ears here?"

"I have my own job to do." I tried to keep the words even and soothing.

Janice didn't want to be soothed. "I didn't kill Lorene. I don't know how to convince anyone of that. Can you?" she demanded.

"Don't you have an alibi? Weren't you having a sales meeting at the time?"

Her expression turned to simple annoyance. "We'd already broken up by the time it happened. Sam wanted to call his wife, and Ross... I don't know where Ross went. I got a drink from the bar and took it up to my room so I could check email and our social media accounts. And I stayed there for the entire evening. But of course, I was alone, so I can't prove anything. I did post on a couple of platforms, but I know you can do that from anywhere." She shrugged.

"I pointed out my cell phone GPS would show I hadn't left my room, but they said the killer probably would've left their phone somewhere else anyway."

She hooked her fingers together in front of her. "The cops think I did it. Everyone knows we disliked each other and were rivals for lots of the same deals. She won some; I won some. Yes, I despised her, but I didn't kill her. She wasn't worth taking that kind of risk for."

"Who do you think did it?" I asked. "You're more familiar with this industry."

She stared into my eyes briefly before turning to watch a group walking by. They didn't look at her products. "Honestly, I don't know. Her nieces had the most motive, but I doubt either of them has the ba—guts to do anything. Plenty of other people here hated her."

"Enough to kill her? But why now? If you had to take a guess?"

"Dave Margolis really wanted the Dougal license. Lorene sucked up to him, seduced him, then stole the deal right out from under him."

The name rang a vague bell in my head. "Is he here at the show?"

"Yeah, the booth's a few aisles down there. He probably hates her the most right now." She nodded to her left, toward the lower numbered booths. "Margolis & Carter. Mostly they import cheap toys from Asia. If you ask me that's the real reason they didn't get the license. Nobody wants to be associated with junk like that."

The light bulb in my head lit up. Margolis & Carter was the booth where they'd found the gun. Did we have a connection between the vandalism and Lorene's murder? I made a mental note to flag Mr. Margolis for Detective

Gilmont. I also wondered if Janice was offering him up to deflect attention from herself.

Before anything else though, I had to say, "I saw your play in the booth this morning. It was well done. Very entertaining."

"Thanks. We hired the best comic actors we could find."

"And they did well. It attracted a lot of attention, too." I hoped the praise would soften her up for the next question I wanted to ask. This one would probably have her frothing, but I ventured it anyway. "Your son said something that intrigued me when I talked to him. He said this should've been a family business, but it isn't."

As I expected her mouth and eyes narrowed and color rose in her cheeks. "That kid! Will he ever learn to keep his mouth shut? He can be such an idiot." She turned blazing eyes on me. "It means nothing. Nothing at all. Wishful thinking on his part. I thought he'd given up those delusions ages ago. This was never going to be a family business. Never."

"Who does own it?" I tried to make my question sound like innocent, idle curiosity. I doubted it would work, but I did get an answer.

"Deveral Torrento. Sam's stepfather."

The answer didn't tell me much. "So, in a sense it *is* a family business."

"In a sense." She snorted. "Sam will likely inherit. Torrento doesn't have any kids from his first wife or Sam's mother. Firing blanks, I suppose. But that doesn't make it a family business."

Once again, the vibes here were confusing. "Why would Ross believe it could be a family business, then?"

She gave me a look cutting enough to scratch glass. "Use your brain. You'll figure it out." She turned away to straighten a stack of sales brochures but looked over her shoulder at me. "And don't bother asking *him*." She turned back to the table. I was dismissed.

I walked up one aisle and down the next for a while, paying little attention to anything around me as I tried to make sense of what she'd told me and figure out how it fit into the bigger picture.

It didn't take a genius to understand what she implied with the last bit. I wasn't sure who I could question about why it didn't happen, though. Would Schmidt himself tell me if I asked straight up? Or should I let Gilmont follow up on it. If he would.

I was drifting back toward the Donneywell booth, and that was okay with me. Even better, as I approached, I saw Jessie sitting at the side, watching while Olivia gave her spiel to buyers focused on Dougal the dragon. Kevin stood in the midst of the group of five people listening.

I caught Jessie's eye as I walked up, but we stayed near the farthest corner to avoid distracting attention.

"Have you got a few minutes?" I asked.

She shrugged. "Looks like it."

"Can you take a break so we can go some place quiet to talk?"

Her expression changed. A quick flash of alarm faded into annoyance. She scanned the booth as though searching for an excuse to decline but found none. After a moment she sighed and said, "Okay. But only for a little bit."

"I'll try to make it quick. How about a drink?" I asked as she joined me in moving away from the booth.

"I could use something," she admitted. "This is my fading time of day."

"Yours and mine both," I agreed. "The Europeans have the right idea with the afternoon siesta."

That drew a brief half-smile from her. We picked up a pair of diet sodas at a stand outside the exhibit hall entrance, then I led the way to a private conference room that should be empty. I unlocked it and invited Jessie in. "I hope it doesn't feel like an interrogation room. But it's quiet and private, two things in short supply around here."

Jessie looked around. "Comfortable chairs, too." She headed for one of the padded leather seats and plopped into it. "If you don't mind if I kick my shoes off and put my feet up on another chair for a while, you can ask me all the questions you want."

"It's just the two of us and I won't tell. Heels are both blessing and curse."

"More of a curse right now," Jessie said. She kicked off her pumps and turned slightly away so she could put her feet on the chair next to her. She sighed. "That feels so good."

We both took long drinks of the sodas. From the look on her face, she relished the cool, sweet, fizzy liquid as much as I did. She set the plastic cup back on the table and said, "I'll answer what I'm sure is your first question. I didn't kill Lorene. I might've wanted to occasionally, but I lose more than I gain from her death. I'll probably be out of a job once the show is over and the cousins take charge of the company."

"I didn't think you did. Whoever killed her must have either hated her, stood to gain a lot, or been seriously afraid of her to take the risk of killing her in such a blatant way."

"Good points." Jessie stared at me. "I heard you solved a couple of other murders that have happened here."

"It's not something I brag about. And not something I really wanted to do. The first time I only did it because the police were looking at the wrong person. The second…"

"You saw the murder happen is what I heard."

"Heard it happen, actually. I was on the phone with the victim when he was killed. It was horrible."

"Dear Heaven."

"Right. I found the body, too."

"Double Dear Heaven."

"After that I felt an obligation to figure out who killed him. I had to, for my own peace of mind."

She gave me a curious look. "Do you feel an obligation to figure out who killed Lorene?"

"Not really. It would be good for business if we could, since there's all sorts of gossip going around about her death. And I don't like the idea of a murderer getting away with the crime. But I'm only asking questions out of morbid curiosity." I didn't mention Detective Gilmont wanted me to keep my ears open. It wouldn't win any fans and not much co-operation.

Jessie gave me a straight, pointed look that expressed her doubts without saying anything, but then she shrugged. "I didn't kill Lorene, and I don't know who did. I know a lot of people who might have wanted to for various reasons."

"The witch queen?"

"She's on the list."

"You said you don't know who she is, but I'm betting you can take a guess."

Jessie's lips quirked. "It's only a guess. But, yeah, I have an idea."

I waited, but she didn't continue, so I prodded, "Will you share it?"

She grimaced. "I don't know anything. But if I had to guess? That woman at Carrie Classics. Janice something. I can't remember her last name."

"Langley?"

"Right. That's it. She and Lorene butted heads several

times. At an open reps' presentation a couple of years ago, they got into a hair-pulling, eye-clawing battle. I think it took a dozen people to pull them apart."

"Do you know what it was about?"

"There was some license Lorene badly wanted, but somehow Janice got to it first or outbid her or something. They do similar product lines, so they were always in competition."

"Which was apparently what happened in reverse on Dougal the Dragon," I said. "But if it's been going on that long, why would she suddenly get angry enough to kill her now?"

Jessie shook her head and took a long sip of her soda. "Good question. Beats me."

"How did Lorene find out about the Dougal franchise being up for grabs?"

After a moment's thought, Jessie admitted she couldn't remember. "But the more important question might be how she knew what to bid. She had to outbid the competition, but not by so much that it would bankrupt the company to produce it. Lorene didn't confide in me much, but I know money is tight. We'll sell piles of them and probably make a good profit, but the cash flow from older lines has gone down and I think she was already over-extended on credit. She was managing it, though."

"What about now? Is there something important in the works they might both be going for again?"

The young woman frowned as she thought. "Not that I know of. Lorene usually told me when she was going after an important deal, but I can't think of anything currently pending. But there was—"

"What?"

Alarm flashed across her face. "Nothing. It wasn't anything important."

"Jessie, I need honest answers."

She shook her head. "I'm trying. Lorene said something about someone owing her money for something. I just told you she was short on cash since she'd invested all her capital in Dougal. That happened when I opened a note to her I wasn't supposed to."

"What did the note say?"

"I don't know. She snatched it away before I could read it. She said it was a personal matter, but the envelope had a stamped return address for Carrie Classics headquarters. That's all I know about it."

"The note was typed?"

"No. Written by hand. That's why it seemed odd. Lorene didn't seem angry or afraid about it, but she didn't want me to read it."

"You don't know what it said?"

She shook her head.

"All right. How well do you know Janice Langley?"

She looked surprised. "Barely at all. She and Lorene were at odds pretty much all the time. She came by our booth a couple of times at other shows. She could be sarcastic and cutting. Nasty. But I don't know anything about her personally."

"What about Olivia or Angelina? They're the ones who benefit most from Lorene's death, and it sounds like neither has a solid alibi. Could one of them have hit her with the car?"

Jessie frowned. "I wouldn't say it's impossible, but honestly, I don't think it's likely. Neither one of them is ambitious enough or ruthless enough. I guess if one of them was pushed into a corner somehow… Maybe if they needed money bad enough and thought they could sell the company?" Her mouth curled into a grimace. "I don't know.

Neither of them seems really worried, if you know what I mean."

"Is it true Lorene bailed out Olivia's company?"

"Yup, but it's also true Olivia paid her back. Lorene helped with Kevin's college expenses, too, but she'd planned to do that all along since she had no kids of her own."

"Does Kevin have any motive?"

Jessie froze for a moment, then sighed. "He'll inherit some of the business through his mother, and Lorene left him some money. But I don't see Kevin killing anyone for it. He's way too nice."

And you like him too much to believe it possible. I kept the thought to myself.

"Does he work for the company, too?"

"He helps out when he can. Mostly he's working on a graduate degree in Economics. Lorene approved. They talked business sometimes."

I didn't see anything further to learn there, so I changed topics. "What was the 'Hartford' thing? Olivia said something about it to Angelina and it clearly wasn't good."

Jessie looked blank this time. "No idea."

My phone pinged with a text message. I glanced at it briefly. I needed to wrap this up. "Can you think of anyone else here who might have a motive?"

Jessie made no attempt to hide her disdainful laugh. "Half the people here. I already told you Lorene would do whatever it took to win. She stepped on a lot of toes in the process. But if you're asking for a person with a specific reason, I can't tell you who it might be. Just that there were plenty of people who hated her or were angry at her, and some who were afraid of her."

"Afraid? Why?"

"Can't say exactly. Really. It's just the way people have acted sometimes."

I tried to think of a way to pin her down to specifics, but I was out of time.

She drained the last of the drink and sat up, wincing as she stuck her feet back in the three-inch-heeled pumps. "I need to get back to the fray. Thanks for the drink and the chance to get off my feet."

I gathered the trash and followed her out, letting the door lock behind me. Janelle's message had said, "My office. ASAP." A demand like that rarely meant anything good.

FIFTEEN

Friday

I WASN'T SURPRISED to find Scott and Craig were already in Janelle's office when I got there, but I didn't expect to see Detective Gilmont occupying one of the chairs. He stood when I came in and offered me his seat. I took him up on it. Scott brought another chair from the next office so everyone could sit. The four of us formed a semi-circle in front of Janelle's desk.

Once we'd all settled, she said, "I told Pete, Detective Gilmont, about the threat the association received. We have no idea if it's related to the murder, but it might be, and we have to take it seriously. He wants to talk about what we can do to help keep the event safe since the Association does not want to cancel it. He also has a few things he can share with us about the murder."

Gilmont turned to face us as he spoke. "I'll start with the murder. We managed to trace the vehicle that was used. It's a rental SUV, and it appears to have been stolen from a parking lot nearby and returned there afterward. The renters are a group of product reps from Japan here for the show. They didn't even realize it had been borrowed until I went to talk to them about it. Only then did it occur to the driver it hadn't been parked in the exact same way he'd left it the previous day. The keys were in the ignition and still there when he went to get it."

"You're kidding," I said. "He left the keys in the car? In Washington, D.C.?"

Gilmont rolled his eyes. "I know. But there doesn't appear to be any connection between any of the reps and the victim. Only one of them recognized the name until he reminded the others of some creature named Dougal." His lips quirked in a brief grin.

"There is minor damage to the front of the vehicle, and we've impounded it to check for fingerprints and trace evidence inside from the driver. A video camera in the parking lot shows a figure in a dark, loose coat, with a hood pulled over his or her face approaching it, the car leaving the lot, and returning about thirty minutes later. Unfortunately, the viewing angle doesn't show a face. All we can say is that the driver was medium to slightly above average height, maybe medium build, and moved at a deliberate pace. No limps or slumping or any other obvious identifiable traits. We tried to trace the driver's path on foot after he or she left the vehicle, but we lost them in an alley a block to the south of the lot."

I groaned inwardly. Medium height and build could be just about anyone.

"I've talked to everyone I know of who had any relationship with the victim," Gilmont continued. "At this point all I can say for sure is a lot of people didn't like her. I gather she had affairs with more than a couple of the men here and wasn't above using sex to get information or favors. The only people with obvious motives are her two nieces and both could fit the general description. I can't establish an alibi for either, but neither of them seems to me ambitious enough or desperate enough to kill for the money. The business is profitable, certainly, but the victim worked hard for the profit. Her net worth looked good on paper, but a lot of that was tied up in the company. Her will leaves all her assets divided equally between the nieces, with a decent bequest to her grandnephew. I believe that's Olivia's son? I haven't had a chance to talk with him. I understand he's now here?" He looked at me for confirmation.

"He is," I said. "I saw him earlier. He couldn't have been responsible for the vandalism, since it happened before he got here. But we don't know if it's the same person." I was thinking out loud.

"Right. I'll need to talk to him anyway." Gilmont scribbled a note on a pad he took from his pocket and looked at me. "That's what we've got at this point. Heather, your take?"

"Pretty much the same as yours. The two nieces don't seem to have the moxie or the motivation to do anything so drastic. Jessie, the girl who worked for Lorene and knows them better, said the same thing. Unless you can find a different motive, I don't see them doing it. There was a mention of a 'Hartford thing' between Lorene and Angelina. I'll see if I can find out what that was, but I assume you've already done background checks on them."

"They're in process," Gilmont said. "But so far nothing of any interest has turned up."

"I have another name for you to check out. Dave Margolis." I explained why he should follow up.

Gilmont scribbled a couple of notes. "Will do. Anything else?"

"I was talking to Jessie right before I came up here, and one thing she mentioned struck me. She said a lot of people here had reason to be angry with Lorene or afraid of her. I didn't have time to follow up with her on it, but I will. We'll never be besties or anything, but I think we've found some common ground and she'll talk to me. It was the 'afraid' thing that grabbed me because it seems like a stronger motive for someone to kill her."

"Why would they be afraid of her?" Gilmont asked. "Was she threatening someone?"

"I don't know. I haven't heard she was, but who knows? I'll try to get names from Jessie."

"Okay. What about the vandalism?" Gilmont went on. "I don't see any reason to think they're related to the murder. The gun thing is interesting, but it wasn't vandalism so I'm not sure it connects to anything."

"Except both are rare occurrences," Janelle answered. "Very rare. And the fact that we've had both at this show raises red flags."

Gilmont shifted in the chair. "I understand, and I've talked about the incidents with Scott, but neither of us sees any obvious link. And I don't know that there's much you can do about it other than trying to figure out who's responsible."

My mental antenna perked up. Gilmont and Scott working together was a new development and I wondered what it meant. But Scott's next words pulled me away from those thoughts.

"We're doing what we can," Scott said. "The guy reviewing the tape thinks he's spotted the drone pilot. When I talked to him, he was trying to verify and get a closer look."

"Good." Gilmont flipped his pad to a new page. "Let's talk about the threat to the awards event tomorrow night. I know it's hard to assess how serious it is, but given the other incidents here, I think we need to take it at face value."

Janelle nodded. "What do you plan to do?"

"We'll have a team sweep the place for explosives or hidden weapons before the party starts. I've talked to the hotel, and they will have extra security on hand. The Association is hiring a couple of extra security people, too. The message doesn't indicate what form the threat might take, so we have to keep our eyes open for anything out of the ordinary."

He looked from Janelle to me. "You two have been to enough of these kinds of things to have a good idea what would be unusual. Before dinner, circulate as much as possible, keep your eyes and ears open. I suspect if anything is going to happen, during the awards presentations would be the target time, when most everyone will be present. People will be circulating back and forth to restrooms and outside for smokes even then, though, so I suggest none of you stay seated. Don't draw attention to it, but keep moving around, watching for anything unexpected. And if you do see something suspicious, call it in. Don't try to stop anyone yourself."

"You'll be there?" I asked.

Janelle inclined her head. "He'll be there as my escort," she said.

We broke up. I had a reminder on my phone to look at the registration database for GlamourThings, so I went to my desk while Scott headed to the security office to check on the video.

A few minutes' work at the computer showed the company had requested two badges, one for Emilia Grinkoff, and one for Josef Grinkoff. So, the man roaming around the floor and hiding behind the curtain was likely her husband. Why did she deny his presence to me if he was legitimately registered for the show? That made me even more curious about him.

As I headed down to the show floor, I couldn't help thinking about what a malicious mind might plan for the

Awards Gala. A bomb was my nightmare scenario, but probably less likely than a shooting or other sort of attack. Still, home-made bombs were ridiculously easy to construct. I shivered but shook it off as I walked toward the Donneywell booth again.

A group of buyers again surrounded Olivia Donneywell, and another two spoke with Angelina when I arrived. Jessie and Kevin stood off to the side, watching the group and speaking in low voices to each other. I hated to interrupt the cozy scene, but I did anyway, walking right up to the pair of them.

"Jessie," I said, "I need you for a couple of minutes. It's urgent."

Reluctance showed on her face, but Kevin said, "I'll wait."

I drew her off to the far end of the aisle, where it was reasonably quiet. "I'm sorry to interrupt, but there have been some developments in Lorene's murder case. I need to ask you for a favor. Can you give me a list of anyone here who you think hated or feared Lorene? Don't worry if you don't know any specific reason for it. Also, a list of any men you know here at the show who had an affair, however brief, with her."

Her expression went tight. "Is this for the detective investigating the case?"

"Yes. But no one will know the names came from you. I'm asking at least one other person for whatever gossip he knows, so it won't be all you, anyway. If anyone asks, we'll tell them the information came from multiple sources."

"Okay. Give me a few minutes. I honestly don't know who might have been afraid of her, just that I'm pretty sure some people were. But the men she had affairs with—I do know some of them." She rattled off a few names and Margolis was among them. A couple of others sounded familiar, though I met and talked to so many people at the shows, I couldn't sort out who they were. "Those were the ones I can think of right offhand," she said. "I know there are others… Can I text you later?"

"Absolutely." I gave her my number. "The sooner the better, though. The show only runs for a couple more days and once it's over, it's going to be much harder to resolve."

"Yeah, I can see that. Whoever did it is almost certainly here right now."

I agreed and thanked her, then headed over to the *Juvenile Playthings News* booth. It was almost five, and I hoped I could catch Daryl Hilderman before he left.

He and another man were straightening up piles of papers as I arrived. They both smiled. Hilderman recognized me and introduced me to their advertising manager.

"Can I borrow you for a few minutes?" I asked Hilderman.

He looked puzzled but said, "Sure. Things are quiet here right now. A lot of people are leaving to get ready for parties tonight. Will you be going to any of them?"

"Not tonight. I occasionally do, but after long days here I mostly want to go home and put my feet up. I'll be at the Awards Gala tomorrow though. I assume you will be, too?"

He huffed a harsh laugh. "Of course. It's the biggest event in the industry each year. In fact, we're going to livestream the awards ceremony. All our staff will be there."

I turned and he followed me down the aisle. "Do you want to sit?" I asked.

"Heck, yes."

We went back to the same conference room where I'd met with Jessie earlier. We grabbed water bottles from a service in the hallway before going in and settling into chairs.

"I need your help," I said, after we'd each had a long pull on the bottles. I explained about the investigation into Lorene's murder. "This isn't exactly professional for either of us, but I need to get some gossip from you. Specifically, I need to have some idea of anyone you know or suspect had an affair with Lorene Donneywell who are here at the show."

He stared at me for a moment, and I could almost see the calculations going on in his brain, so I wasn't surprised when he said, "I'd be willing to trade what I know for what you know."

"Right now, the little bit I do know was shared in confidence by the police and I can't discuss it. But I'd be willing to offer you an exclusive interview once the killer is identified or the case is closed by the police."

"And if they don't close it? If the case drags on and on?"

"When is the deadline for your next edition?"

"We're putting out show special electronic newsletters every day. The big one will be the one the morning after the Awards Gala, of course. Next week we'll do a print and electronic edition rounding up all the biggest news from the show. Since it's print, too, the deadline is Monday at five."

"Call me Monday at two and I'll give you everything I can."

He set down the bottle after taking another drink. "Deal. Let me ask this... You want to know about who she had affairs with. Does that mean the police think the killer was someone at the show?"

"I can't speak for what the police think," I said, trying to be careful. "But logic suggests that's most likely."

He nodded. "True. So, as far as people I absolutely know she's had affairs with... There's only one because he told me so himself. In confidence, of course." He stared at the bottle for a moment, then looked at me. "You will keep the source of this information confidential?"

"Yes. I promise. We just need it to point to possible suspects. And you're not the only person I've asked. I've already promised others I wouldn't divulge their names."

"Okay. The one I know for sure is Ed Fendrick of Fendrick and Drury Imports. I haven't seen him here so far, but his name is on the attendee list. I can't see him having any reason to kill Lorene over it. It happened a couple of years ago. He told his wife and begged forgiveness. Apparently, she gave it. I don't think there's anything there to worry him."

"How about any others you've heard about?"

"There are a few. Some rumors are more reliable than others, though."

"Start with the most reliable," I suggested.

"Okay. Two that seem likely are Tom Oakley, a rep who works with several companies here. I've seen him in the Spallford booth the past few days."

I made notes on my phone as he spoke.

"The other would be Sam Schmidt at Carrie Classics. You met him at our booth the first day of the show."

"I remember. He's already admitted to an affair with Lorene, so he isn't trying to hide it."

"Still," Hilderman said. "Given they do similar product categories, it's at least interesting."

"It is. But I can't see an obvious motive. He doesn't seem to have the same anger at Lorene that Janice did."

"Okay." He stopped to think for a moment. "Other possibilities are Oliver Handley, Len Goldfarb, and Zander Santiago. Goldfarb's VP of marketing at TinWood Productions and Santiago's with Barrio Arriba Toys."

The first name on his list rang a bell. "Oliver Handley? The electric vehicle company?"

"Yup. Bit of a scandal there, I think, but I've only heard vague whispers about it. Might've broken up his marriage."

"Interesting," I said. "Anyone else?"

"These are even less certain. Maybe just guessing by some people." He rattled off a couple more names and I added those to my list. None of them sounded familiar.

"Can I ask you about one more bit of gossip?"

"Go ahead."

"Carrie Classics. What's the story between Janice Langley and Sam Schmidt?"

"Ack. Them."

"Yeah," I agreed.

"There was a rumor of an affair between them, but I don't know. I don't get any feeling of chemistry there. Not now, anyway. Besides…"

I raised my eyebrows and waited.

"This really is just rumors I've heard, but… A bit of background. Carrie Classics is owned by Schmidt's step-father, something Torrento. Can't remember the first name. Anyway, the old man stepped back from running the company a while ago and left Schmidt in charge. He didn't have any kids of his own, so he pretty much adopted Schmidt, and everyone assumes Schmidt will inherit the company when the old man dies. A couple of years ago there was a rift, though. I've never heard what caused it, but some speculated Schmidt had an affair and maybe even wanted a divorce. Torrento was…is partial to the current Mrs. Schmidt and put the kibosh on it." He put his hands up. "That's all I can tell you and I don't even know how much of it's true."

He glanced at his phone. "I need to be going," Hilderman said. "We have an editorial meeting over dinner tonight."

I thanked him and said goodbye as we reached the doors of the exhibition hall. People were pouring out and we had to fight the tide to make our way back inside.

Hilderman had given me a lot to think about. Schmidt had admitted he had an affair with Lorene Donneywell, but he'd suggested it was more of a brief fling than the kind of relationship that would break up his marriage. But if he'd had an affair with Janice Langley and it got serious, it would explain a lot. It certainly made sense of Ross's complaint about how it should've been a family business, presumably *his* family's business. The situation was messy and ugly, but I didn't see how it connected with Lorene's murder.

A couple of other things Hilderman mentioned puzzled me as well. I was still wrestling with the fact that Handley might have had an affair with Lorene Donneywell and what connection there could be with the vandalism at his booth when my phone buzzed with a message from Scott.

"Come up to the security office. Have something to show you."

SIXTEEN

Friday-Saturday

I LEFT THE exhibition hall, joining the flock on the escalator down to street level, but at the bottom, I turned to the left and took the elevator to our offices. Scott came out of the tiny, dark video room when I pushed through the door marked "Security." I tried to gauge his excitement, but Scott didn't wear his emotions openly. He signaled for me to join him.

A dark-haired man in his early forties sat at the desk in the video room. He turned to watch me enter.

"This is Greg Watkins," Scott said. "He does free-lance video and graphics editing. He's a whizz at it."

Greg offered a winning smile and held out his hand. "Scott exaggerates." His handshake was warm and firm.

"Not much." Scott nodded to one of several screens showing various views of the exhibit hall floor. Some had live motion coverage of action in the aisles, while others, mostly at the sides, showed frozen views. The one Scott indicated featured a still shot of a row of small booths at one end of the cavernous area. "Greg thinks he's spotted the drone pilot."

Greg pointed to a different screen. "This was tricky because I had to match up the times on these views. We first caught the drone here." He picked up a pencil to point to where the drone flew low under a table in a booth that featured snap-together wooden toys. "I can't locate a start point for it any earlier than this, but I figure it was hidden somewhere in the vicinity, probably in an unobtrusive place where it could sit unnoticed. I've combed through the video and can't isolate it any earlier than this or see anything that's recognizably someone placing it. The thing might've been flown to that position so low the cameras didn't catch it. Anyway…"

He let the video run for a few minutes, using the pencil to trace the drone's movement. "It settles over here, in a corner beside one of the snack booths behind a couple of trash cans. Nothing happens for almost an hour." He tapped on the keyboard which fast-forwarded the video. "Here is where it starts its rampage." The drone rose, startling people nearby, and sailed up and out of the picture. "I didn't try to follow it, since based on the times, we pretty much know what it did next."

He pressed more keys. "Look at the next screen up. I've done some time matching on a number of feeds and I came up with this." The screen above the previous one showed an aisle a couple over. Based on the booths I saw, it might be the twenty-two hundred aisle. People moved in and out of the screen; some stopped to talk, others fingered merchandise; and a couple glanced at their phones. Greg stopped the video, stood up, and used the pencil to point out a shadowy figure wearing a dark suit and a broad-brimmed cowboy hat pulled down far enough in front to hide his face. He held up a phone and appeared to be typing something into it.

"Is that the drone pilot?" I asked.

"We think so," Greg answered. "He stands there for nearly ten minutes, working on the phone. Unfortunately, the camera angle means we can't see what's on his screen, so we can't say for sure that's what he was doing, but he's the only one whose phone interactions match up closely with the drone's actions, timewise."

I stared hard at the figure. "Can you blow him up any?"

"I can zoom in some," Greg said. "But I can't get much more detail. He turns toward the camera a couple of times, but the hat keeps his face hidden."

I stepped closer to the screen. I guessed they assumed the figure was a man based on the clothes. But the shoulders weren't all that broad and the suit coat disguised the hips, making it impossible to be sure. Medium height, probably in the five-foot-ten, five-eleven range. Something about the form seemed familiar, but not enough to help with an identification. I was reminded of the play I'd seen at the Carrie Classics booth, but the hat wasn't the same as any of the actors wore.

"If he stood there that long, wearing a cowboy hat, some of the exhibitors on that aisle might've noticed him," I said, thinking aloud. "That hat—it's not out of line at a toy show but still might draw attention. And they could have seen his face."

I looked at Scott, who said, "We'll start questioning people on the aisle first thing in the morning. It's not a lot, but at least it gives us a lead."

My stomach grumbled, demanding food.

Scott grinned. "Quitting time. Thanks, Greg. I appreciate it. Send your bill."

"Will do. Nice to meet you," Greg said, turning to me. "I hope you can catch your guy before he creates even more havoc."

"So do we all," I agreed.

The three of us walked out of the office and through the now-quiet building to the exit for the employees' parking

area. Greg went to his car, and I walked with Scott around
the building while he checked locks on all the doors. Once
that was done, we headed for dinner in Bethesda. D.C.
traffic was heavy at quarter past seven on a Friday night.

The restaurant was crowded, too, but after a short wait
at the bar, we were seated. Once we'd ordered, Scott said,
"I forgot to mention this earlier, but I think we've figured
out how the vandalism at Handley took place with no one
seeing or hearing it."

"Really? I'm all ears."

"Ears. That's the key. Noise and chaos. Distraction and
cover for the sound of the vandalism. Your adventure with
the dog made me think of it. I kept wondering and worrying about what else was happening around us while everyone was focused on the runaway pooch."

He was enjoying keeping me in suspense, stretching out
the story while we waited for food. "Actually, it was Greg
who found it, but I suggested what to look for. He had to
comb through a bunch of video, but he came up with it. On
the other end of one of the aisles Hanley borders, a large
shelf of boxed toys was knocked over, creating a huge mess
and racket. We must've been somewhere else at the time
since neither of us heard it, but plenty of people in the area
did, and gathered in the aisle to look. Some even pitched
in to help clean up." He sounded genuinely surprised by
that. His ex-cop cynicism kicking in.

"Anyway, while that was going on, someone used the
distraction to scrape the side of the display car. Quite a
few people passed close enough to do it while heading toward the melee down the aisle. We couldn't focus in tightly
enough to see someone damage the car, but it wouldn't have
taken much. An arm extended with a key or small hook in
hand could easily manage it in passing."

The server showed up with our dinners. Scott waited while we took the edge off our hunger, but I could tell from his expression he had more.

After we'd each made inroads into the food, I said, "Okay, give over. You've got something else. You look way too pleased with yourself. Did you figure out who did it?"

"Maybe and no," he said, taking a long pull from his beer. "I looked closely at the Handley car and at the pictures you took of it. After watching the video, I'm convinced the vandalism wasn't done by anyone in the booth. The scrapes were on the side facing the aisle. Someone passing by could have gouged the car, but it would've taken two swipes to create the level of damage we saw. And in watching their space during the melee, I noticed one person who appeared to pass the booth twice within a couple of minutes. Unfortunately, that's the good news. The bad news is he wore a baseball cap pulled down low, so we didn't get any view of his face. But, if I were a betting man, I'd put a lot of money on him being the same person we saw piloting the drone."

"Okay. He's being very careful to keep his face hidden. What do we know about him? Are we even sure he's a 'him'?"

"From what I've seen I'm pretty sure it is. Five-ten to six-feet-tall, medium build. I'd guess fairly young, but that's just a guess. Not elderly, certainly, but could be anywhere up to and into middle age."

I took a sip from my wine glass. "Eliminating all the women and older men, that still leaves you with probably a quarter of the exhibitors here."

"I know. But it feels like we're making progress. We might even get an ID tomorrow."

"Do you think the threats to the event tomorrow night are from the same person?"

Scott thought for a moment. "If there's more than one, they've got to be working together. Anything else is too much coincidence."

I sighed. "Yeah. I thought I'd seen everything in the years I've worked here, but we've never had anything like this random vandalism happen."

Scott's expression darkened. "There are a lot more things that could happen. A lot more bad things. Be glad they haven't and pray they don't."

"I don't want to imagine."

He shook himself, casting off the momentary black mood, and reached for my hand. "Sorry. Some of those places I try not to go."

"And you definitely don't want to share."

He gave me a sudden sharp look. Did he hear some resentment in my tone? Maybe. Sometimes I wanted to yell at him about keeping secrets. "I have a few dark places of my own, you know. I could understand."

He frowned.

He knew I had some dark places I did my best to avoid revisiting. He knew mine but wouldn't share his own. I swallowed hard. "It hurts that you keep things from me. Probably important things. You put me off and deflect when I ask about them. You don't trust me enough to share."

He straightened and drew a sharp breath, then took my hand. His expression looked pained, eyes and lips pressed tightly together for a moment. "I will tell you everything. I promise. But it's…you may not want to continue our relationship after. Give me a little while longer."

My stomach twisted into a knot, and I pulled my hand away. "That bad?"

He barely moved, barely breathed before he said, "Depending on how you look at it."

"I don't know what to say to that." I wanted to scream at him to just tell me and let me draw my own conclusions, but he wouldn't, and I wasn't ready to create a scene in a public place.

He took my hand again. "I wish I could convince you to believe in me."

"I hope you can." We stared at each other briefly, then he released my hand and sighed. He looked at his plate but neither of us felt like eating anymore.

Picking up the check, Scott asked, "About tomorrow night? What time do we need to be there?"

"Officially cocktails at six, dinner at seven. The awards program will start around eight, then there's music and dancing afterward. I'll bring a change of clothes in the morning since I doubt there will be time to go home."

Scott nodded. "I'll do the same. We'll want to be there early." I could hear the strain in his voice.

Scott drove to my apartment. To break the uncomfortable silence between us, I needed distraction. "I'm drowning in gossip. Collecting a list of people Lorene had affairs with and some who hated her. It makes me feel slimy."

"Police work is often like that. With any luck, there will be a nugget in it to point Gilmont in the right direction."

"Yeah." I leaned back and tried not to think about anything until we got to my place. Normally he'd come in for a while. That evening he stopped at the door. He leaned in to kiss me, but stiffened and watched me, waiting. I desperately wanted the kiss—and more—but wasn't sure I could handle it. He settled for giving me a peck on the cheek.

Before turning to go, he offered to pick me up the next morning since I'd be wrestling a garment bag as well as my usual tote, which would be awkward on the Metro.

I wanted to slam the door behind me.

I rolled around in bed for an hour or so, wondering what he might've done that could be so bad he wouldn't want to tell me about it. A couple of possibilities occurred to me, and I didn't even want to think about those. When I fell asleep my dreams were filled with ugly images of bombs exploding in crowded places. I woke with a sense of foreboding so thick I wanted to burrow back under the covers. Dread hung over me like a dark cloud as I showered, brushed my teeth, dressed, and put on makeup.

SATURDAY GOT OFF to an odd start. The ride to work was awkward with Scott and I not having much to say to each other. Or actually there was a lot I wanted to say but didn't dare. Not today, anyway.

Then I got a text message from Janelle asking me to handle a problem in the fifteen hundred aisle. She gave me booth numbers to check in with but no indication what the issue might be. Janelle herself hadn't arrived by nine. That wasn't like her, and I wondered what she was up to. Scott had left to check in at the security office when we arrived, and I didn't see him again before I headed downstairs.

Nothing appeared out of the ordinary when I got to the fifteen hundred aisle. Everything looked like business as usual in the area. In the booth Janelle had indicated as the origin of the complaint, two men and a woman talked to potential customers and showed off samples of electric road race games.

The space to the left of them featured snap-together construction sets that looked fascinating. They had a table spread out where potential buyers could try them out and I was tempted. You could do so many different things with all those intriguing pieces. I pushed that away.

To their right, a company that sold a target practice game

also had a demo set up. A series of computer monitors hung on brackets along the back of the booth showed garish and constantly moving, changing targets. At the front, close to the aisle, two long tables held the plastic pistols that fired soft foam darts. The tips of those activated a touch-sensitive screen, causing a raucous explosion if it hit one of the wiggly, rushing target creatures. The result was an intriguing cross between an old-fashioned, arcade-style target contest and a video game.

Anyone passing could try out a handful of foam darts by dropping a business card in the fishbowl.

Half a dozen people currently stood at the tables shooting at the targets. Most of the projectiles hit the curtain backdrop and fell to the floor. Cheers went up from a small group surrounding one shooter when his dart struck a target and an on-screen fireworks explosion ensued. At least they had the noise turned down.

But one of the other shooters had bad eyesight or bad aim or both. Not only did his dart fail to hit the target, it didn't even stay in the booth. Instead, it flew over a low set of shelves into the construction set area, narrowly missing an eye of one of the people assembling some strange construction from the snap-together parts. Being foam, the missile likely wouldn't hurt anyone, but it scored high on the annoyance and distraction scales.

All three of the people with exhibitor badges in the construction set booth turned and glared over at the dart gun set up. An older, well-dressed and beautifully groomed Black woman picked up the dart and began to march over to the next booth.

I said, "Wait, please," as she moved past me. "Center personnel. Let me handle it."

She stopped, turned to me, and checked out my badge.

"They're driving us crazy with these things. I've got a box full I've collected that I'm not giving back, but they brought an unlimited supply."

"And didn't think about how many people had really bad aim."

"You said it."

"I'll talk to them," I promised her. "This needs to stop."

"Good luck with that." She nodded to her fellow employees. "We've each had a 'talk' with them in the last couple of days, and you can see how much good it's done."

"Understood. But they will have to listen to me. I could shut them down."

"You'd get lots of cheers from the area if you did. We're not the only ones they're annoying."

"I'm sure. But we try to work with people before we resort to the nuclear option."

"Good luck," she said.

I made my way to the front of the dart-gun booth and stood at the side. One of the two young men in the area had watched my conversation with his neighbor and didn't look surprised when I approached. He made his way toward me.

"Bill Evans," he said, holding out a hand. Bill was young, probably about my own age of twenty-six, dark-haired, medium height, and lean. His wide hazel eyes held a guileless, innocent look that I didn't buy for a minute.

I identified myself and shook his hand.

"I suppose you've gotten some complaints about our darts straying?" he asked.

"You think? So, I have to ask, what are you doing about it?"

He looked around helplessly. "What can we do? Not everyone has great aim, so those darts will go in unpredictable directions. But they're foam and not firing at a high velocity so they're not hurting anyone."

"If one of those were to hit someone in the eye, it could cause damage," I countered. "But beyond that, they're a nuisance and a distraction. They interfere with your neighbors' business, and that's one thing we don't tolerate."

"We don't want to do that. Honestly. But you don't have side walls on these booths, so what can we do?"

"I can think of several things," I suggested. "Build up stacks of boxes to create a barrier. Get some wall panels and I'll get some of our maintenance people to work with you on setting them up. We can put up a pole at the front on each side." I used my foot to show him where the covered socket was. "And a crossbar from there to the back so you can hang a sheet or swatch of fabric to catch most of them." I looked around as another dart flew into the booth on the far side. "We understand you can't stop all of them from escaping, but you've got to make an effort to contain most of them."

He folded his hands together and cracked his knuckles. "How soon do we have to get it fixed?"

I checked my watch. Nine-thirty. "I'll have someone from maintenance here to help set up the poles shortly. You'll have to supply your own sheets or curtains, but I can suggest a couple of stores nearby where you can buy something quickly. I'd like to see some effort made to fix the problem by lunch time."

"Tomorrow's the last day of the show anyway," he said.

"I know. But your company can be barred from future shows if you create a hazard or nuisance and make no attempt fix it."

Alarm crossed his features. "Listen, if we get it fixed, no one else needs to know that there were complaints, right?"

"No one else…like who?"

"Like the owner of the company. Our dad. Rick and I"—
he glanced to the other young man talking to a potential
customer—"talked Dad into trying this. He's old-fashioned
and prefers to rely on the reps making the rounds—which
is okay, don't get me wrong! But Rick and I had this idea
for taking sales to the next level by doing this show. We're
betting that if people get a chance to play with the product they'll be hooked and want to feature it in their stores.
And so far, it's worked. We have stacks of orders. But if
Dad hears there were complaints…he'll lower the hammer
on the whole thing."

I held back a grin. "If you have barriers on the sides by
noon, he'll never hear a thing. Hold on a minute." I called
maintenance and explained what I needed. They promised
someone would be there shortly.

As I ended the call, an ear-splitting racket crashed
through the buzz of commerce in the hall, drowning out
everything else. It sounded like the sirens on several play
firetrucks turned up to their highest levels, so loud it was
painful.

I tried to lean in to remind the young man in the booth,
"Lunch time. I'll be checking." I doubted he heard me. People all around clapped their hands to their ears. I headed
toward the racket.

SEVENTEEN

Saturday

THE NOISE ECHOED around the area, multiplying as it bounced off the roof, and throbbed painfully against my eardrums. It probably did come from several toy ambulances or fire trucks, but why the heck didn't someone turn them off?

As if reading my mind, the sirens cut off one after the other, leaving a strangely echoing silence in the wake of the last. The rumble and chatter of many voices filled the sound vacuum within seconds. I even heard a few curse words tossed in the direction the sound had originated from.

A crowd collected around the booth at fourteen-twenty, where towers of boxes held twelve- to twenty-inch trucks of all types, including ambulances, fire trucks, and polices vans. An unboxed toy truck sat at the top of each display. That seemed to confirm its likelihood as the source of the racket.

Another thought struck me as I reached the edge of the mob, determined to push my way through. *Distraction. This was another distraction.* I backed hastily and turned to look down the aisle. More people headed toward me, but none appeared to be trying to damage anything. Most looked puzzled or curious. *A hat.* The vandal had worn hats to conceal his features for his previous efforts. *Look for someone wearing a hat.*

No one I saw wore any kind of headgear. The crowd blocked my view of the aisle in the other direction. Moving against the traffic stream, I worked my way to the end of the aisle and around and up fifteen hundred. Still didn't see anyone wearing a hat or acting furtively. I got to the center cross aisle and went to where it intersected with fourteen hundred. Staring back down from the other side of the crowd revealed nothing interesting either.

I went to the next aisle, thirteen hundred, stopped there in the middle, and looked both ways. People still poured into the area, some with such aggressive expressions I feared they wanted to have more than just words with the party responsible for the maddening noise. But no one acted suspiciously or wore a hat—until I spotted a figure in a hoodie disappearing around the farther end of the aisle.

I chased after him, but at least fifty feet separated us. He turned toward the right when he reached the front, but almost immediately disappeared from my sight. I crashed into one gentleman who gracefully held me upright and accepted my hasty apology with a smile, then just avoided a woman with a large, heavy shoulder bag. By the time I made my way to where I'd seen him last, he was gone. I glanced all around, but he could've left the exhibit hall by the main doors, headed up the next aisle, or crossed to any of several beyond it. There were too many ways he could've gone and too many potential hiding places. I wasn't going to find him.

As I conceded defeat, a high-pitched scream sliced the air from somewhere nearby. It sounded female. I couldn't tell whether the cry was from terror or pain or possibly both. I raced to the vicinity, pushing others out of the way

in my haste. A crowd gathered around a booth that featured dolls of all sizes, shapes, colors, and modes of dress.
I shoved my way through them to reach a group of three
men and two women in the center. One of the men had his
arm around a woman who sobbed softly, while one of the
others examined a shelf of dolls on the side.

I glanced at the area quickly, turned to the people in the
center, then looked back at the shelf as what I was seeing
penetrated. A line of baby dolls maybe a foot high sat in
a row...with grotesque damage to their faces. Despite my
concern for the crying woman, I walked to the side for a
closer look. I hadn't been wrong. Something had made the
doll's faces melt and run, leaving them grossly disfigured.
Liquid slid down foreheads and cheeks along with melting
rubber or vinyl, and I reached out to touch it.

"Don't!" The man standing there grabbed my arm. "I
think it's some kind of acid. It burned Liddy when she
touched it."

I pulled out my phone and called Scott. He answered on
the second buzz. Since I could hear a clamor in the background, I guessed he was on the next aisle over. "The noise
was a distraction," I said without waiting for him to say
more than his name. "Right around the corner at thirteen
sixteen. Need you here right away."

I ended the call and looked at the man who'd stopped me
from touching the doll. "When did this happen?"

"Just a few minutes ago. Liddy saw it first. She touched
it and it burned her hand."

"Did you see who put it there?"

"No. We didn't know anything had happened until Liddy
noticed the dolls didn't look right."

I wanted to question him further, but I had a more important priority. I walked over to the group huddled around the

woman. She no longer wailed but was still gasping, clearly in pain. One man poured water from a bottle over her hand. Another opened a second bottle and handed it to the first when the bottle he held ran out.

"Center personnel," I identified myself to them. "How bad is it?"

"Bad enough," the man pouring the water said. Two of the woman's fingers looked bright red, the skin rough and uneven in a patch that spread from the tip to beyond the second knuckle. "She needs medical attention."

"We have first aid facilities downstairs." I called down to alert the nurse on duty that we were on the way and what she'd be dealing with.

Scott ran up behind me. "What's going on?"

"Some kind of acid. Ask him." I pointed to the man who'd stopped me touching the dolls. "I need to take her downstairs to first aid. We'll probably need the fire department."

The woman continued to gasp and shake. One of the other men took off his suit jacket and draped it over her shoulders. I told him to help her and follow me. Moving as fast as we could, I led the way out of the exhibit hall, down the escalator, and around to a little-used hallway where the first aid room was the second door on the right. The nurse, Marcie, met us as we came in. "I've got an ambulance on the way." She looked at the woman's hand and guided her to a sink in the corner where she ran cool water over the burned area. Marcie dragged a chair across the room and sat the woman down while she kept the water running over her fingers.

"What happened?" I asked.

I'd expected the man to answer, but the woman, Liddy, spoke first. "Someone poured acid on the Kolsburg dolls." She sounded outraged. "I didn't see who did it, but several people were near them. There was a crowd running down the aisle when those sirens started blaring, so several people passed near the dolls, but I didn't see anyone do anything like this. When the rush stopped, I noticed one of the faces seemed to be doing something odd, bubbling, with the surface kind of melting. I made the mistake of touching it and—it felt like my fingers were on fire."

"Did you see a man wearing a hat or hoodie near the dolls?"

The woman frowned. "I didn't notice anyone particularly."

The paramedics arrived then and took over the woman's treatment, rolling her out on a gurney within a few minutes.

Once they'd left, I asked Marcie, "Was that necessary?"

"The paramedics? Absolutely. A chemical burn, no matter how small, is serious and needs more than just first aid care. Plus, there's a potential for shock. So, yeah, it was."

I thanked her and headed back up to the exhibit hall with the man who'd accompanied us. He in turn thanked me for the help, and added, "We were never actually introduced. Keith Scranton."

"Heather McNeil," I said. "Assistant to the director of the Market Center. I'm so sorry this happened. I can't imagine why someone would want to do such a thing."

"I have no idea either." He shook his head, looking puzzled. "Nothing like this has ever happened to us."

"Could someone have a grudge against the company or an employee?"

Scranton spent a moment considering it. "Not for anything I know about. I'm vice president of sales, and I should think I would be aware if there were issues."

"You haven't done anything controversial lately? Take-over bids or your CEO making unpopular political statements?"

"Not at all."

We got back to the show floor and headed for their booth. The thirteen hundred aisle was blocked off where authorities had set up stanchions with plastic tape that said, "Crime Scene—Do Not Enter." Three people in Hazmat suits checked the carpet and shelf with electronic devices. They moved the dolls on that shelf to a container that looked like an oversized drink cooler. The lid was still up on it and as we watched one of the people in protective gear dropped another doll into it.

At my side Scranton made a sound that fell somewhere between a moan and a cry of protest. "The acid wasn't on all of them. Just a few."

"True," I answered. "But the others might have been contaminated. They can't take a chance on it."

A pair of police officers talked with two of the other people I'd seen in the booth while Scott was with the third. Janelle stood at the side looking on, until she turned and saw us approaching. The others looked up as well when we got closer.

"They've taken Liddy to the hospital to get checked out," Scranton told his co-workers. "She should be okay, but the nurse said any chemical burn had to be considered serious and needed treatment she couldn't give."

A police officer approached, but he mostly wanted to talk to my companion. Scott and Janelle pulled me to the side.

"She's okay?" Janelle asked.

"I think so. She may have a scar, though. I don't know how acid burns work, but Marcie did."

Janelle watched a man in protective gear shut the container with the dolls and sighed heavily. "This is going to be a mess. I've already notified our lawyer and insurance company. We'll cover her medical expenses, of course. And any loss the company suffers. Do you have any idea what happened?" She looked first at me and then to Scott.

I glanced at him as well.

"As best I can tell, someone dropped acid on a couple of the dolls while everyone was distracted by the sirens. No one saw it. None of them saw anything out of the ordinary until the woman—Liddy—noticed that they looked odd. I'm going to ask Greg if he can come back and look at the video."

"Good idea," I said. "Tell him to look for a figure in a hooded sweatshirt." I explained about the man I'd seen and tried to chase earlier.

"Will do," Scott said. "In the meantime…"

Janelle had turned aside to say something into her phone. She ended the call and faced us again. "Maintenance is ready for clean up or to help us set up a temporary booth at the front again, if needed."

We'd done that at a previous show when I'd found a body in a private area of a booth and the police had sequestered that booth and the neighboring ones until they'd processed the crime scene. It had been a huge amount of work and hassle. I hoped we wouldn't need to repeat the effort. Especially not so close to the end of the show and with the awards gala that night.

"What was the story with the siren blaring?" I asked Scott as Janelle went to talk to the officials working on the cleanup.

"Just as you guessed." He gave me a small wry grin. "Distraction. Someone turned on the sirens on several display trucks and left. I didn't have time to ask many questions, but the first two people I asked didn't see who did it. Our vandal is quick and sneaky."

"They didn't see anyone even after the first one started blaring?" I found that hard to believe.

Scott shook his head. "Apparently not. I'm going to try again with them."

"Could it be more than one person?" I asked.

Scott gave it a moment's thought. "Could be, but I think not. We haven't seen anything on the video to suggest another person. And having two people doubles the chances of getting caught. I think we've got just one; one who is very clever and very careful."

I looked around. "Very disturbed, too, I think. This is all just so… I don't know. Nasty. Creepy, even. The other things were bad, but they were just things. This time someone got hurt."

"I don't think that was intentional," Scott said. "I think he was just going for vandalism again. The woman touching the acid was an unfortunate side effect. Collateral damage, if you will."

"Are you kidding me?" His blasé attitude stunned me.

"Hey, I'm giving you the vandal's perspective. Not mine. Personally, if I had the guy in front of me right now, I'd—" He stopped and drew a breath. "I'd like to do things cops and security officers aren't supposed to do."

"And I'd be cheering you on."

"In any case, there's something else about this attack that worries me. You were getting at it when you said this was nastier. It is. Melting dolls' faces feels more direct and personal than knocking over block statuary and scraping the sides of cars. It's escalating."

"And it doesn't feel so random," I added. "There's a method to this madness. He's creating distractions in the vi-

cinity of where he wants to attack. Plus, he had to have prepared specifically for this with a supply of acid." I stopped
and studied the undamaged displays of dolls in the booth.
"What's the point, though? What is he accomplishing?"

"Good question." The voice came from behind, startling
me. I whirled to face Detective Gilmont. "And is this all
related to the murder of Lorene Donneywell?" he asked.
"If so, how?"

"We'd all like to know the answer to that," I said. "I
didn't expect to see you here."

"Janelle called me. Someone was injured, which makes
it an assault." Gilmont studied the activity for a moment
before asking, "What happened?"

I told him what we knew about the attack.

Janelle joined us after a moment. "Fortunately, the actual
amount of acid was small. We'll rip out part of the carpet
and remove the shelving, but we don't have to move them
out of the booth. The fire department will rope off the spot
and put some special stuff on the floor, then maintenance
will have to clean it up."

I breathed a small sigh of relief, glad we wouldn't be
going through the temporary booth trauma.

"Do we have any idea who was responsible?" Janelle
asked.

"For whatever it's worth, we're reasonably sure it was the
same person behind the other vandalism incidents," I said.

Janelle rubbed her temples. "Not worth much without
a name."

"I know."

Scott spoke for the first time in a while. "I was trying to
find one when I got the call to come here. I've talked to a
couple of people who noticed the man in the cowboy hat before the drone incident, but so far no one has seen his face.

I need to go back to the booth with the fire engines. I can't believe no one there saw him when he set off those sirens."

Janelle waved him off. "It's probably the best use of your time right now." She turned to me. "I've got requests for you, too. Minor things, I think." She pulled out her phone and forwarded a couple of texts to mine.

Before I left to take care of those, I told Gilmont, "I've got some names for you. I need to compile the list, though."

"The sooner the better," he said. "We'll keep working it after the show, but the more people we can talk to now, the better. By the way, Margolis is out. He has a solid alibi."

"Okay. We can cross him off the list. I'll send you the other names as quickly as I can."

I wasn't sorry to leave the remaining chaos in the thirteen hundred aisle behind. The two assignments Janelle had texted were both, as promised, minor. A company in the five hundred aisle had some problems with their electrical connection. I put in a call to maintenance for an electrician. In the seventeen hundreds an exhibitor was running low on sell sheets and needed the name of a nearby printing company who could fill an order quickly. I keep a list of local vendors and merchants on my phone for such situations, so I could recommend a place right away.

As I walked away from the booth, I got a text from Jessie with a couple more names. I headed upstairs to compile the list in relative peace. To avoid running into anyone I'd have to talk to, I went to a back staircase. The effort failed when Dennis Michaelton peered out of a door from the shipping area and called me. "Heather, do you have a minute? I need to ask you something."

I wanted to tell him I was in a hurry, but he deserved better. "I have a couple of minutes."

"Good. It won't take long. I just wanted to ask you about

Scott Brandon. I know he's a former cop and you're dating him, so I hope this doesn't offend you, but…what is he
doing here?"

I stared at him, puzzled by the question. "Working security as far as I know. Why?"

"A couple of things about him don't add up. He's too
bright and sharp to be working in a place like this. He's a
cop. A real one. And why does he want to go through my
shipping records? What's the point in that?"

"I don't know. There are things he doesn't tell me. Some
things that seem to be off limits. Have you asked him?"

"I tried, but he brushed it off and changed the subject.
Every time I've asked."

Scott was good at that. I'd experienced it, too, especially
early in our relationship when I'd tried to find out why
he'd left the police department and started working here.
He'd hinted that he'd left under a cloud but refused to talk
about specifics.

"I don't know what to tell you," I admitted. "I've asked,
too, and gotten the same results. But I feel sure he has a
reason."

"I'm sure of it, too," Dennis said. "I just wish I knew
what it was."

EIGHTEEN

Saturday

I COULDN'T HELP thinking about Dennis's questions concerning Scott as I made my way up to the office level via a back staircase. I didn't often use the steps since I got plenty of exercise hoofing my way around the exhibit hall while shows were running, but it did give me a way to go up without having to deal with anyone else.

His doubts echoed mine and reinforced the misgivings I'd shared the previous night.

I'd wondered about Scott since he first started working here back in March. At the time he seemed an unlikely candidate for the job of house security officer. Most of our security people were either older and no longer able to meet the physical requirements for a police job or younger people who couldn't pass the tests to get in.

Everything about Scott—the lean, fit body, quick mind, careful control of his emotions, ability to project authority and confidence—suggested a man who'd make a better than average police officer, and probably one with a good chance for a quick climb up the bureaucratic ladder. Even if he had, as he'd suggested, done something to sour his relationship with the Metro D.C. Police Department, there would still be plenty of other opportunities for a man with his looks, intelligence, and bearing. Better paying and higher status opportunities.

So why was he working here? He hinted at something in his past so dark I might not want any relationship with him when I knew. What could be that bad? Had he killed someone? Taken bribes? Committed some other crime? Or was it something else entirely? My stomach twisted into a painful knot.

I'd stopped questioning his reasons for being here after we started dating, and now I wondered if I'd fooled myself into thinking he stayed because of me. I'd been attracted to Scott from the moment I met him. He's good looking and he's got that alpha male confidence that appeals to most women. A significant dollop of compassion, a wry sense of humor, and at least the appearance of solid integrity added up to something close to my ideal man. All indications suggested the attraction was mutual. I think I have a realistic view of myself. I'm reasonably attractive, both physically and personality wise. But I'm no *femme fatale*, and to think my presence would be enough to keep a man like Scott in a low-paying, low-status job for very long was likely kidding myself.

This was the first real sign he might have another agenda in being here, though. He'd done his job and done it well since he started. He'd been supportive and helpful several times in bad situations. Everything I'd seen from him indicated he was a decent man of solid integrity.

After our conversation the previous night, I now had to ask myself just how devastating the truth might be and whether I could handle it. Scott wasn't the first man I'd dated or even the first I'd been attracted to. Those guys had been fun, a good time, even a passing infatuation. None of them had lured me into wanting a deeper, longer-lasting relationship the way Scott had. Maybe he was right that I would prefer ignorance. But he knew me well enough to understand that would never work for me.

I choked back the incipient tears and pushed aside those musings when I got to my office. I'd deal with it later.

There were a few other people in the administrative section, but none too close. I nodded but didn't stop to chat. At my desk, I sat down and opened a new document on my computer.

Consulting my memory of what people had told me, the notes on my phone, and a couple of texts, I compiled a list of all the individuals known to have had an affair with Lorene Donneywell, suspected of it, or who at least had reason to dislike her. There was some overlap on the lists, and I ended up with eight. I had company names associated with all but two. Googling gave me the other two.

After crossing Margolis off, reducing the number to seven, I stared at the list. Some of the names were familiar. Leaving off Margolis and Schmidt, I'd had recent interactions with two other companies associated with people who had some relationship with Lorene Donneywell. At least, I thought so with one of them. I consulted the show floor plan and verified that the acid had been dripped on dolls displayed in the Saroyan Designs Inc. booth. Saroyan Designs was owned by Clark Saroyan, whose name had been given to me by both Daryl and Jessie.

Oliver Handley's name also appeared, the man whose prized miniature car had been scratched a couple of days ago. This had to be more than coincidence. The only vandalized company that didn't appear on the list was Playblox. I checked the registration database for their team members present but couldn't establish any connection for them. Still, two out of three? Maybe three out of four, if I included the hidden gun at Margolis & Carter?

I grabbed my phone and texted Gilmont, telling him I needed to see him as soon as possible.

A message from Janelle came in a few moments later. "We're coming up in a moment. Bringing lunch."

I hoped the "we" meant her and Gilmont. A lot of the booths were offering lunches for attendees today, so I anticipated she would find some interesting food.

In the meantime, I studied the list again, struggling to keep my thoughts from straying to Scott and our relationship. I checked my email inbox for distraction but found nothing of any interest.

Janelle came in shortly, bearing plates of something that emitted a wonderfully savory aroma. "Barbecue," she proclaimed. Gilmont entered with another plate and a plastic squeeze bottle full of a reddish liquid.

I grabbed my lists and followed them into her office. "I hope that tastes as good as it smells."

It did. The food lived up to and even exceeded the promise of the aroma. I ate more than I needed, but my nerves were on edge. "Scott still trying to find the vandal?" Janelle asked when we'd taken the edge off our hunger.

I paused a moment. "As far as I know."

After swallowing the last bite of my barbecue sandwich, I pulled out the two lists I'd made. "Speaking of that, I think I've found a connection between Lorene Donneywell's murder and the vandalism."

Gilmont set down his fork and looked at me. "Oh?"

I handed him one of the two lists. "These are the names, with their companies, that people have suggested either had an affair with Lorene or had reason to dislike her." I gave him the second. "This is the list of companies who have been vandalized during the show. That we know about," I added.

Gilmont studied the lists for a moment, then his eyebrows rose. He looked up and handed the sheets to Janelle.

"You think the same person who killed Lorene is behind the vandalism?" Gilmont asked.

"Kind of looks like it," I said. "At least, there's some sort of connection."

"Can't argue with that." He held out his hand and Janelle passed the lists back to him. "But one thing you learn in police work is there are lots of kinds of connections and not all are what you think. The same person could be behind both the murder and the vandalism. But there are other possibilities."

I wracked my brain but didn't have any ideas. "Like?"

Gilmont tapped his fingers on the arms of his chair. "I admit coincidence is unlikely, but it is still a possibility. Diversion? Trying to get us to look in the wrong direction for the killer? A setup? Some bigger plot? This is interesting and I'll definitely pursue it, but it's not conclusive. It does give us a direction, though, and that's helpful."

"Diversion does seem to be the vandal's favorite trick. But I still don't see how it fits together," I said. "Why kill Lorene and harass the people who either had affairs with her or might have a motive for killing her themselves?"

"I wish I could answer that, but I don't have any more idea than you do." Gilmont stood. "I'm off to ask more questions."

He left and I helped Janelle clean up the lunch mess. "Good choice," I told her. "That was delicious Anything else I need to look into this afternoon?"

"So far, I don't have anything. Have you checked in with Scott? See if he has any clues."

"Will do." I pulled out my phone to text him and drew a deep breath. "Are you as worried about tonight as I am?"

Janelle crumpled a napkin left on the corner of her desk and tossed it at the waste basket. The balled-up paper bounced off the rim and onto the floor, so I picked it up and dropped it in. "At least as worried," she said. "This mess is making us look bad. I'm not minimizing the damage to our clients and the awfulness of murder when I say that. But the Center facilities are my responsibility and we're failing our exhibitors right now."

"We're doing everything we can."

Her expression lightened. "I'm not implying anything about my staff. You're all going above and beyond to try to figure this out. I know that. If I'm criticizing anyone, it's myself. What have we missed in our regulations? What could we do differently to prevent things like this?"

I gave it a moment's consideration. "Probably nothing. Human beings will be human beings, and that means you can't predict all the possible ways they'll come up with to create chaos."

"Good point."

My phone beeped with a text from Scott. It read, simply, "Nothing so far."

Janelle's desk phone rang as I looked up to relay Scott's message. I waited while she listened and got ready to move when she said, "I'll have someone there in a few minutes to help." She hung up and looked at me. "Twenty-four forty. Some kind of food disaster. I'll have maintenance meet you there."

"You don't suppose it's another vandalism?"

"I hope not. I don't think so, though. This sounded more like an accident. It certainly wouldn't be the first time for that."

"True."

I headed back downstairs, fortified by barbecue but hoping I could pick up another cup of coffee. There was still a lot of day ahead. I also seriously hoped the food problem wouldn't turn out to be another vandalism incident. We'd had plenty of accidentally overturned coffee urns, soda dispensers, and chafing dishes at previous shows. Not to mention a malfunctioning popcorn machine drove me crazy back at the Gifts and Accessories show a few months previous. A cotton candy dispenser threatened the Center's power grid at last year's toy show. The hot pad "failure" at the Chef's Kitchen extravaganza two years past cleared the show floor with the smell of burning plastic.

A small crowd had formed at the twenty-four forty booth, which featured kid-sized sporting equipment, including freestanding basketball hoops on poles tucked into weighted floor stands. Those, along with stacks of boxed baseball mitts, football helmets, and soccer goals, had been moved to the back to make space for two tables across the front of the booth.

As I nudged my way through the group, I realized most of the people standing there were actually in line for food from the two chafing dishes still on duty. A pile of egg rolls steamed gently in one while the other held a noodley mix of something that smelled delightful. If my stomach wasn't already full, I'd be fighting the urge to get in line myself. But duty called.

Another food pan had been tactfully moved to the end of the table. It appeared to have held a mixture of rice, broccoli, and bits of meat, much of which was now strewn all over the floor of the booth and into the aisle. Credit to the booth operators, the line of people had been moved away from the messier section, and a man and woman attempted to corral the straying food with a broom and sheets of paper.

I identified myself to the person who appeared to be in charge, a woman with nicely styled graying hair and careful makeup that made the most of her good bone structure. "Our maintenance people will be here in a moment," I told her. "What happened?"

"Crowd accident." She nodded to a person behind me. "Someone got bumped, and she bumped into the chafing dish. Someone else tried to help her and made it worse instead, and the dish went flying." The woman sounded more resigned than angry about the incident. "I'm so sorry about the mess."

I assured her we'd seen worse, and it was nothing but the truth. Within moments, the squeaky wheels of the cleaning cart announced the approach of Mark and Tim from the maintenance department. I didn't have to do much explaining, which was a good thing. My phone buzzed with a text message as I was telling them what had happened.

Elation surged through me when I saw the message: "I've got him."

NINETEEN

Saturday

JOY FADED WHEN I noticed the sender's name and realized the text wasn't from Scott or any member of the staff. It came from the man in the booth across the aisle from GlamourThings.

I had to assume he'd cornered the man they'd been complaining about or had at least talked to him. I didn't mind having an excuse to take off, though I did stop at a booth on the next aisle to snag a gourmet coffee, hoping the double-shot latte would help see me through the rest of the day.

The sounds of a scuffle reached me as soon as I turned onto the six hundred aisle. Loud voices, mainly. The loudest one sounded like Emilia Grinkoff, which was no shock. A couple of deeper male voices rumbled in response. A chair squeaked. Odd grunts mixed in.

Once again, I had to nudge my way through a circle of people two or three deep to get into the booth. A large man with dark hair, mustache, and dark eyes sat in a chair, surrounded by several men and women, all trying to talk to him. One had a hand on the large man's shoulder, pushing him down when he tried to rise. Emilia Grinkoff yelled at the group around him, a steady litany of "Let him go. He doesn't understand. Let him up."

The man who'd first complained about the GlamourThings booth, Don Miskoski, according to his badge, fired questions in a too-loud voice.

I moved into the group. To get everyone's attention I announced loudly that I was "Heather McNeil, Center Administration." The talking and shouting ceased for a moment, then Miskoski looked at me and said, "This is the one who's been sneaking around and cutting through booths."

The dark-haired man tried to rise again and made a few grunting sounds. He wore a badge that identified him as Josef Grinkoff, an exhibitor with GlamourThings Accessories. He met my eyes with a pleading look and uttered more of those incoherent noises that might have been attempts at words.

His hands moved wildly, making a series of strange gestures, and his expression grew increasingly disturbed. An internal light bulb fired up as I watched. Those weren't random movements. He was trying to speak with his hands.

I looked at Emilia Grinkoff. "He's deaf, isn't he? Can you talk to him? Tell him that we don't want to harm him or hurt him."

She banged the flats of her hands against the sides of her head in a helpless, overwhelmed gesture. "Yes, he's deaf. And a little slow, too. I don't do sign language very well. He's my brother and he just came to live with me four months ago. He was with my mother in New Hampshire, but she passed on last March. He had nowhere else to go unless I put him in some kind of home. He doesn't deserve that." She pressed her lips together for a moment. "But I had to be here for the show, and I didn't want to leave him at home alone. I'm learning some sign language, but it's not easy."

She turned to Josef and made more hand gestures. They

must've been less than clear to him because he frowned and gestured back, ending with his hands raised in a questioning way. They went back and forth for a couple of minutes until he nodded an affirmative to something she said.

"Please let him be," she told the others around. "He says he'll be calm and not try to run away." She stared at the man who still had a hand on Josef's shoulder, glaring at him until he lifted it. Josef remained seated, looking around at us in a puzzled way.

His expression changed as he glanced over us at the aisle. He smiled in response to the approach of a pretty, blonde young lady. I recognized her as the woman who'd denied seeing Josef the day before. Her name tag said she was Terry Caswell. She stopped and swept her gaze around the group. After taking a step toward us she paused until I signaled for her to join us. My suspicion about her was confirmed when she made hand gestures to Josef that made him smile again.

"You know sign language," I said.

"My sister is deaf, so I grew up with it." Terry "spoke" a few more words to Josef with her hands, and he responded in kind. "Poor Josef, he's so overwhelmed by all of this. He's not used to crowds of people and all the…action. And he can't communicate with anyone. He doesn't know what to do or how to act. He's completely lost. He was so happy yesterday when we met and he realized I knew sign language, but I also have a job to do here, so I can't give him as much time and help as I'd like to. Right now, I'm trying to tell him to calm down, that it will be okay, and no one wants to hurt him."

"Thank you. I'm glad you're here," I said.

Emilia turned to her also. "Please, can you tell him I'm

KAREN McCULLOUGH 183

sorry I brought him to all this chaos? I didn't know what else to do."

The girl relayed the message and waited while Josef responded. "He understands and is happy you brought him. He can't make sense of what's going on here and why people get upset with him."

"He doesn't belong here," one of the men still surrounding his chair said. "He's not a salesperson or in the business."

"GlamourThings paid for their booth just as you did and put him on the list of registered exhibitors," I told him. "I understand he's been disruptive, but given the challenges he has, I think we can cut him some slack. Now that we know what's going on and have someone who can talk to him, we'll explain what he can and cannot do, in a way he can comprehend. I think that will fix the problem."

I didn't actually have my fingers crossed, but if you can do it mentally, those digits were all tangled up. I considered my next move. One way or another I needed Terry, the only person around who spoke sign language. We could probably hire an interpreter from a service, but it would take time. I turned to her. "Is there any chance I could borrow you for half an hour or so to go over some things with Josef? I know you have a job here, but could your employer manage without you for a bit? Long enough to have a quick talk?"

"I haven't had my lunch break yet. Let me see if it's okay to take it now."

"I'll buy you lunch," I said, "And Josef, too."

She took a moment to text someone and got a ping back quickly. She smiled at it. "I'm good to go. By the way, there is another native deaf person here at the show. Jennie Taylor at Carrago Toys. She has some speech but mostly she's a brilliant artist. Carrago does art and craft kits, so she does amazing demos of what's possible. After we're finished eating, I'd like to take him to meet her. Would that be all right?"

"It's fine with me," I told her and turned to Emilia. "Would you mind?"

The worry lines on her face had eased over the last few minutes. "Not at all. It would be good for him to meet another person he can talk to."

Before we left, I turned to the other exhibitors in the booth. "The Center apologizes for any disruption Josef has inadvertently caused. I'm sure Ms. Grinkoff will be extra careful to be sure nothing else her company does disturbs your operations." I stared hard at her.

Her slight nod told me she'd received the message, so I let it ride at that. The complainers appeared mollified enough to return to work. A large, tight group of buyers picked that auspicious moment to head down the aisle. I left the exhibitors to the business of wooing and schmoozing.

I'd already eaten but I still had the as-yet-untouched coffee I'd picked up earlier. An insulated cup had kept it warm. I took Josef and Terry downstairs to the food court area and let each choose where they wanted to eat. Terry got a burrito and Josef pointed to a burger image on a sign. The lunch rush had ended by two-fifteen, though people still sat around. We carried the food to a quiet corner table. I sipped my coffee—perfect drinkable temperature—while they took the edge off their hunger.

Once they finished eating, I used Terry as a translator to impart to Josef that he had to respect the boundaries of other people's booths. She spent some time telling him about it, then reported to me she was having to explain to him what was going on with the show and why everyone was there. Apparently, his sister had never made clear what being at a trade show would involve or suggested how he should act. I could tell from his facial expressions when he began to understand the situation.

"He's not slow at all," Terry told me. "That's his sister's impatience and misunderstanding. He doesn't have all the background information hearing people do. Plus, his up-bringing was pretty sheltered. Once things are explained to him, he gets it. No one told him this wasn't just an in-door fair or a carnival like others he's been to in his life, so it's no wonder he thought he could just roam wherever he liked. Now he realizes this is business, and the people in those booths are showing off their products for other busi-nesses to buy. When I told him it was more like a market than a fair, he understood."

More hand gestures passed between them, and she added, "He says he's willing to do whatever he can to be helpful."

My phone buzzed with a message from Janelle concern-ing a problem at another booth.

"I appreciate the offer," I told her. "Right now, the most helpful thing would be for him to assist his sister with run-ning her booth."

She passed that on, and he nodded. A few more hand gestures and Terry turned to me. "He also wants to thank you for helping him and settling the problem with those other people. He was afraid they would hurt him or have him taken to jail."

"He's welcome." I smiled at him to reinforce the mes-sage, and he returned it with a grin that made him look at least ten years younger and much less fierce.

We cleaned up the wrappers and tossed them and my empty coffee cup in the trash. Terry and Josef left to meet this other woman who used sign language, while I went to the two thousand aisle, where, halfway up, a couple of men were engaged in a noisy argument.

Fortunately, the issue concerned the quality of some merchandise a buyer had ordered at the last show. By the time I arrived the senior person on site was taking care of the problem, so I just asked them to keep the noise down and left.

Two texts came in while I was with them. One from Scott simply read, "No luck." The other was from Olivia Donneywell asking if she could talk with me. I checked my watch. Three-ten. Just a couple of hours until I had to get ready for the Awards show, and I was starting to feel frantic. But I couldn't think of anything else useful to do in the meantime, so I told her I'd be there shortly.

On my way to their booth, I stopped by the dart gun game space. Maintenance had set up vertical poles on either side at the front, with horizontal ones running from the front to the back. Someone had draped striped sheets on both, creating de facto walls on either side. It wasn't perfect and wouldn't stop every wayward dart, but sometimes you had to settle for good enough.

TWENTY

Saturday

OLIVIA WAITED FOR me at the Donneywell booth. I didn't see Angelina, but Jessie and Kevin were talking with prospective customers. Olivia and I left them to it. We followed the enticing aroma of coffee to a booth offering a variety of gourmet brews and snagged a couple before I led the way to a small, unoccupied conference room.

Once we settled and had each sipped some very hot and strong java, Olivia gave me a hard stare. "Jessie said you sometimes help the police. They talk to you. I need to know—do they have any idea who killed Aunt Lorene?"

I debated how much to say and decided to go with vague. "I don't know. They don't tell us everything."

"The police still think one of us did it. And they're wrong." Olivia set down her coffee cup and chewed her lip. "Aunt Lorene wasn't the easiest person to get along with, and a lot of people disliked her. I understand why. But she was good to me. She bailed me out of an unexpected financial crisis with my business and helped with Kevin's university tuition. I owe her a lot. I hate to think whoever killed her will get away with it. That's not right."

"I agree it's not right. I know the police are doing their best and I think they might have some leads. But honestly, that's all I know. I can't say if they're even close to making an arrest."

She hesitated again. "Jessie said that you've solved a couple of mysteries here in the last few months."

Oh, no, we're not going there. Please.

But she did. "Time's running out for the show. Is there any chance you could look into it, maybe try to find out who did it? I know you've talked to Jessie and others around here."

"That was just to collect information for the police." I sipped my coffee, hoping it would help me think. More caffeine might not have been the best idea. I was already wound up. But the day had a long way to go, and I'd need every bit of help to get through it. "I'm still gathering ideas, and time's running out. If you'll help with all the information you can, I promise to do my best."

Olivia nodded slowly. "That's all anyone can ask. What do you want to know?"

"Would Angelina have any reason to want Lorene dead? And what was the 'business in Hartford'?"

She swallowed a mouthful of coffee the wrong way and started coughing. When she got it under control, she said, "Angelina? No way. Why would she? Not because she stands to inherit anything. I mean she gets a share of the business, but administration isn't her strong suit. She was better off with Lorene alive. Lorene would sometimes pay her a consulting fee to help design marketing stuff."

"The Hartford thing?" I prompted.

"Well, that was a bit of bad luck and maybe some bad judgment on Angelina's part. About ten years ago, she took a job with a sleazy insurance company, and the Feds caught them in some illegal shenanigans. Unfortunately, Angelina was mixed up with them. Lorene paid for a good lawyer, and he proved Angelina was an unknowing dupe in the scheme. She ended up having to testify against her boss, but that was it."

"Angelina didn't get any threats about her testimony?"

"Not that I know of. It's not like these guys were the mob or anything. They were a pair of stupid putzes looking for easy money."

I considered the incident but seeing it as relevant to Lorene's murder involved serious stretching. "Someone mentioned Kevin had gotten into a few scrapes and Lorene bailed him out."

Olivia's eyes narrowed and lips pressed together for a moment before resuming a more neutral expression. "Kid stuff. He got in with a couple of bad influences in high school. Nothing really bad like drugs. But they did some stupid things…and got caught."

"What kind of stupid things?"

"Kid stupid things. Splashed paint on a school wall. Maybe put salt in the principal's gas tank. Kevin swears that last thing wasn't him. Anyway, they did some community service and that was that. He straightened up, went to college, and did very well. He's in a graduate program now."

Vandalism. How much was she trying to protect her son? Was there a connection to what happened here? Not obvious, but worth keeping in mind.

I had other questions while I had her here and cooperating. "You said you knew some people disliked Lorene. Are any of them here that you know of?"

"I haven't been here long," Olivia said. "And the booth has occupied all my time, so I have no idea who's here or not. But I would assume they are, since they were mostly business competitors."

"Give me some names if you can."

"I'm afraid I don't remember most of them. But I know a couple of companies that she had dealings with. Unpleasant dealings."

"That will help."

Her face crinkled in thought for a moment. "There's Norwood. I think they do mostly plush toys. And Barrio Arriba. I remember that because the name is odd. Carrie Classics, of course."

"Of course?"

"I'm sure you've heard there was no love lost between them. She and that Langley woman were always in cutthroat competition. There was something between her and Schmidt, too."

"According to him, they had a brief fling."

"I think it might've been something more," Olivia said. "She got a certain look in her eye when she talked about him."

This was new. "What kind of look? Angry? Jealous?"

"None of those. I don't know how to describe it. Predatory maybe? Or possessive? Something strange. Of course, they're a competitor and she got the best of them in the Dougal deal, so maybe that was it."

"I haven't heard this before. I got the impression whatever was between them was over quickly."

Olivia gave me a blank look. "It probably wasn't anything. I'm just giving you my thoughts. Nothing concrete."

I was weighing what to make of that and how to follow up when Olivia said, "I'd better get back to the booth."

My phone buzzed with a call.

Scott. I ignored it until Olivia had left.

"Any luck?" I asked.

"Nope." He sounded discouraged. "I can't believe how many people failed to notice a guy in a hoodie messing with their toys, or someone in a cowboy hat roaming the floor staring at his phone."

"They have other priorities."

"I suppose," Scott said. "Anyway, I thought we better get a bite early. I'm not planning to eat at the dinner. Are you?"

"Not this time."

"Good. Meet you upstairs in fifteen?"

I checked the phone's time. Four-twenty. "I'll be there."

I made one more quick swing across the show floor at the center aisle. The noise level had diminished, and the crowd was thinner. People had begun leaving to get ready for the evening. I swung by the Donneywell booth where I saw only Angelina talking to another woman. I walked past Carrie Classics. Janice and Ross Langley both focused on a group of buyers, toting large briefcases. I glanced at PlayBlox where even the elaborate castle had been rebuilt. Tinstall Machines had a drone demo in progress. Nothing needed my attention, so I headed upstairs.,

Most of the office staff were preparing to leave. JoAnn, our PR person, waved and said, "I hear you're heading for the Awards Gala. Can you make sure I get a list of winners tomorrow, so we can update the displays?"

"I'll do my best," I said. No point in telling her how far down the priority list that task sat. I relayed what Daryl Hilderman had told me about their magazine live-streaming the event.

"Oh, that's great. Thanks. I'll check it out." She shrugged her purse onto her shoulder and left.

I heard voices in Janelle's office and peered in. My boss sat at her desk, while Scott and Pete Gilmont occupied the other two chairs. Both men wore suits.

Janelle looked up at me. "Come in. We're strategizing for tonight. Pete and I are heading across the street in a few minutes to go over the security arrangements. Scott suggested the two of you should get something to eat now so you won't be distracted later. It's a good idea. If you want, I'll take your dress over and leave it with the concierge so you can change there after you eat."

"Sounds good." I looked at Detective Gilmont. "Any other developments?"

He grimaced. "Two more people on your list have solid alibis so I'm crossing them off. Two don't, but I can't establish any motive for either of them."

"So, no progress."

"Crossing people off the list is some progress," he said.

"I guess. Here's another bit that might be worth following up." I related Olivia's admission of her son's history of vandalism. Scott looked interested and Gilmont thoughtful.

"If it was a juvie case, the record's sealed," Gilmont said. "I talked to him yesterday, but I didn't know about that and just asked about his relationship with his aunt. Didn't sense anything off from him, but you never know."

Scott said, "I'll swing by there tomorrow and try to have a word."

"Good. About tonight…" I looked at the others in turn. "I had a thought. If we assume the person threatening the gala is the same one who's responsible for the vandalism, then we need to consider that creating diversions is his favorite tactic."

Janelle and Gilmont both looked at Scott.

"You've already thought of it," I said, staring at him.

"I did. But this guy is clever enough to establish a pattern of diversions, hoping we'll assume this is another one."

I pressed my fingers to my temples. "You're making my head hurt."

Janelle laughed and even Gilmont cracked a grin. "We

still have to take the threat to the gala seriously," the detective said. "And keep the possibility of other options open, too."

"I suppose the obvious is another attack on an exhibitor. But how could he do that tonight?"

"No idea," Gilmont answered. "The building will be locked and should be empty aside from the cleaning crew."

I sighed heavily. "This is all beyond crazy."

Scott stood up. "And you're probably hungry, too. Are you ready to eat?"

"I guess." I turned to Janelle. "See you across the street in an hour or so."

Scott and I walked a couple of blocks to a tapas restaurant I liked. Their small dishes were wonderful, and their flavored sangrías to die for. Unfortunately, I was on duty, so no sangría for me. A shame. My nerves were jangling, which made me regret the drink even more. Aside from worrying about what might happen later, I needed to tackle Scott with the questions I had.

But not before we ate.

We each ordered several small items, lamb bits in sauce, seared scallops, potato wedges, and an artichoke spinach dip for me. Scott leaned a bit harder on the vegetables, but also got a prime beef tips dish. My stomach felt tight, and I hoped I'd be able to consume my share.

"How do we do this?" I asked him once we'd ordered and had each sipped from our water glasses. "Tonight. My gut thinks the threat to the gala is another diversion. But even if it is, how can we know what to pay attention to?"

"If it makes you feel any better, I hired Greg to keep an eye on the video feeds from the exhibit floor tonight. He figured out a way to stream them to his home system so he can watch from there. He'll let us know if he sees any-thing out of the ordinary."

"That's a good idea. It helps. So, we go to the dinner and keep our eyes open there while Greg watches the Center."

He held the water glass and swirled the liquid gently. "It's not perfect. The cameras have limited range and reso-lution. And Greg can only do so much on his own. I warned him the cleaning crew would likely be in there, too." He sounded concerned. "I consulted with Craig about it ear-lier, and it's the best we can manage right now."

"And a lot more than nothing," I said. "I feel better about that. A little. I'm still worried about the dinner. There are so many things that could go wrong. And we might not know about them until too late. Remember the Gifts show awards dinner?"

"I do. The threat to Grantwood. But we misunderstood the threat that night. And probably got lucky."

"Yeah." I sighed.

A waitress arrived with our food. We ate in silence for a few minutes. My churning gut wasn't receptive, but I needed the fuel, so I forced myself to take a bite or two from each of my dishes and try a couple of Scott's. It was all delicious. At least I'm pretty sure it was. My state of mind didn't allow for much attention to taste.

"You know, this is a fun show," Scott said, "despite the threats, murder, and vandalism. I haven't messed around with PlayBlox or GlitterDough for a long time."

"You indulged?"

"For a few minutes each, while everything else was rea-sonably quiet. Made me feel like a kid again. That's what this show should be."

"And usually is." I looked up at him, sensing this chatty mood was meant to distract me from thinking about tonight. I was willing to go along with it. "Aside from the bike, what did you like to do when you were a kid?"

"The usual, I guess. Playing games with my brothers, although those frequently devolved into fights. Building things, some reading." He grinned. "My mom had to put several games away because we always got into arguments over them. That Operation game? The one where you're the doctor, and you have to pull things out without touching anything else? We were always trying to nudge each other or rock the table when the other one had a turn."

"I'll bet you were a noisy bunch."

"No doubt. I'm sure that's why my mom was always chasing us outside to play. We had a basketball net over the garage, and we'd shoot hoops even in the snow. And argue over fouls. Constantly. We were a competitive bunch."

The waitress came to collect our plates and ask if we wanted anything else. I suggested coffee since we still had a long evening ahead and Scott agreed. I let out a long breath. I had no more excuses to put it off.

"I have a question for you," I ventured.

Something in my tone alerted him. He looked at me and his expression grew serious, the light of amusement fading from his eyes. "This sounds ominous. I'm not going to like it, am I?"

"Maybe not. But I still have to ask."

"Okay."

"It's kind of related to our talk last night."

I watched his expression change again, growing wary and possibly a little nervous.

Nonetheless, I pressed on. "What are you doing here? I mean, working at the Center. And please, spare me the glib answers. I talked to Dennis Michaelton, and he had the same reaction to you. You don't fit here. Even if you're not with the police anymore, you could be so much more. You're too smart, too competent, too educated, too competitive, too...everything to be working for practically minimum wage here. No matter how big a difference you had with your previous employer, you could do so much better than this."

He stared at me for a moment, and I could almost see the wheels turning in his head. The waitress returned with our coffees. He waited until she'd departed and I'd added cream and sugar to mine before he asked, "Why bring this up now? When we're facing a serious challenge in the next few hours?"

I struggled to find an answer. "Maybe that is the reason."

"You don't trust me?" He sounded startled and dismayed.

"No. I mean, yes, I do trust you. Mostly. You were the one who said I wouldn't like it when you told me the truth. So, what am I supposed to think? When it comes to doing the job, I trust you completely. It's about *why* you're doing this job."

"I see." The dismay grew even clearer in his expression. "I told you last night I would give you the truth, but I hoped it could wait a little while yet." He took a sip of his coffee, frowned at it, and set the cup down.

"I'm sure. But we do need to have it. It's about us, Scott." I stared into my cup, not sure I could bear to see his reaction. I had to swallow to get words past the lump in my throat. "If there is an 'us.' A real 'us.' I thought we had the beginning of something special. But I can't help wondering... If you've lied about why you're working here, what else are you lying about? Is our relationship real or am I being used?" My stomach was twisting itself in knots again.

I looked at him. The muscles of his face pulled tight as

though he fought some internal battle, or maybe he was in pain. He sighed heavily. "Heather…"

I took a drink of coffee and braced myself. I wasn't going to like his answer. The waitress brought the bill and set it down.

His lips twisted in a grimace. He drew a deep breath and reached over to take my hand. I let him, even though that touch made everything harder. I wanted so much to believe it would all be okay. I wanted him so much. I wanted to be closer to him right now.

His words came out hoarse and strained. "I'm in a tough spot here. But you should know… You are special to me and what we have is important. I will tell you everything. I promise. But this isn't the place and now isn't the time. We can't afford any distraction right now. When we've wound this up or when the show is over, I'll explain everything. You'll have to keep it to yourself for a while, but you'll understand why." He closed his eyes for a moment then opened them and looked at me with so much mixed pain and longing, I wanted to throw myself at him and tell him to forget it all.

I didn't, because getting this sorted out was too important to our future. We sat together, hands clasped and staring at each other for a long time.

Finally, I said, "I'll hold you to that promise."

He nodded and glanced at his watch. "We'd better get going." He took several twenties from his wallet and left them on the tray with the bill.

As we headed back to the Market Center, he said, "Are you ready to switch gears? We need to put the personal stuff out of mind and concentrate on trying to keep the dinner tonight safe."

"Roger that," I answered.

He reached for my hand. I let him take it and hold it as we walked. I just hoped I wasn't digging myself into a hole I'd have a hard time climbing back out of.

TWENTY-ONE

Saturday

As WE APPROACHED the northeast corner of the huge Market Center building, we turned left, away from it, and crossed the street to the hotel entrance. The lobby bustled with activity. Newcomers checked in at the desk; temporary residents came and went; and gorgeously dressed people arrived for the awards dinner.

As promised, Janelle had left my dress bag with the concierge. Once we retrieved it, I retreated to the ladies' room to change while Scott went to check on security arrangements. I promised to text him when I was ready.

I'd brought one of my three designer dresses for the gala. This one, my newest, a dark blue, knee-length sheath with a lace overlay flattered my figure and made me look taller. It called for high-heeled silver sandals to set it off properly, but given how much I'd be on my feet tonight, I opted for more comfortable navy pumps with a medium, block heel.

I pulled my hair back into a bun, leaving tendrils loose on either side of my face, and used more makeup than I normally did, going heavy on the eyeliner and shadow. Twenty minutes later, I decided I'd do and let Scott know I was ready.

His reaction when he spotted me while crossing the

lobby made my breath catch. He stopped short for a moment and his eyes widened. His smile... Not broad beaming approval, but something tighter, delighted and almost pained at the same time, made my heart twist. An expression only a first-rate actor could fake.

He shook it off and came to me. "You look fantastic." He took my arm and tucked it into the crook of his elbow to escort me to the ballroom. We garnered more than a few second glances as we crossed the lobby, with Scott collecting as many—if not more—than I did. His tall, lean frame did great things for a suit.

"You ready to go on full alert?" he asked as we neared the door.

I drew a deep breath and let it out slowly. "I suppose so."

Scott pulled the invitation cards out of his shirt pocket to show to the person standing at the doorway. The young woman gave Scott an admiring smile before handing back the cards and glancing to the next persons in line.

Soft music played from overhead speakers, almost lost in the cacophony of chatter rising from the people already gathered in the cavernous ballroom. Many were lined up at the four bar stations around the room while others stood in clumps, nursing drinks.

I did a quick scan of the area. A stage stood at the far end, to my left, with a broad wood dance floor in front. Round tables topped with white cloths, each set for eight guests, occupied about half the entire space in the middle of the room, leaving wide aisles around the edges where most of the people currently gathered to chat. In addition to the bars serving alcoholic beverages, long tables on two walls provided water, soft drinks, and what appeared to be pitchers of iced tea.

White-coated servers passed through the crowd, bearing

silver trays of canapes. An appealing, spicy aroma wafted from beyond the door to the kitchen. It all looked reassuringly normal. My nerves continued to buzz.

"Let's circulate," Scott suggested.

Keeping my hand on his arm, we walked slowly through the crowd, aiming to circle the room. I recognized some of the people we passed and smiled back at those who greeted me. One stopped me to ask whether the police had made an arrest for Lorene Donneywell's murder, while another wanted to know if they'd caught the vandal. I hated that I had to say no in both cases and assure everyone the police were doing all they could. Scott chimed in to add that there were some leads and clues in both cases, and he thought arrests would happen soon.

Janice Langley and Sam Schmidt passed us going toward one of the drink tables. Both nodded—Janice coldly, while Schmidt's was more diffident.

"That was chilly," Scott whispered in my ear.

"Janice Langley, Carrie Classics. I'm not her favorite person, but she's currently my top bet for the Donneywell murder."

His eyes narrowed thoughtfully, but he didn't say anything more. The interactions I saw all looked normal for a gigantic cocktail party. People stood around in small groups talking. The clumps broke up and reformed periodically. Servers replaced pitchers of tea as they emptied and replenished the supply of cups and soft drinks.

We approached Janelle and Detective Gilmont, who also made a round of the floor in the opposite direction. We stopped for a moment to compare notes.

"There was a crash in the kitchen earlier, probably before you got here," Janelle said. "But it was just someone knocking a big pot off a table. That's the only unusual thing we've seen or heard."

Around us chatter grew louder as the crowd swelled. Some people had already staked out seats at the tables. I saw the Donneywells gathering at a table on the far end. Kevin held a seat for Jessie, then sat beside her. That looked cozy. The thought crossed my mind—did Lorene know there was something between Kevin and Jessie? Had she disapproved? Thin, but it could provide a motive for the murder.

Other people I recognized found tables and sat. Oliver Handley, with his son-in-law and a woman who had to be his daughter, were not far from us. I glanced at my phone. Ten to seven. They should be starting dinner service soon. I still hadn't seen anything suspicious in the room. Several steely-eyed men and women in suits stood at various spots, watching closely as well.

I was surprised when Emilia and Josef Grinkoff entered a few minutes later. I doubted she had any products up for awards. I had to blink a couple of times to recognize Josef in a nicely fitted suit with his hair combed and expression almost friendly.

A woman stepped up to the microphone on the dais and announced, "Ladies and Gentlemen, if you'd please be seated, dinner service is about to begin." Most of the remaining chatterers scrambled to find places.

Scott tapped my arm and nodded to a far corner of the room. "Janelle wants us."

I looked that way. Janelle and Gilmont were talking with a tall, beautifully dressed, but visibly upset older woman.

My gut twisted. Something had happened.

We didn't run, but Scott and I wasted no time scooting across to join them. Gilmont tipped his head toward the door, and we continued out of the ballroom, into the lobby. They followed with the woman.

Janelle led us to a conversational seating group in a quiet corner, though none of us sat. "This is MaryAnn Webster, president of the Juvenile Play Products Association." She introduced Scott and me to the woman.

"We have a problem," Janelle continued, but then looked to Ms. Webster to take over.

"The awards are missing." The woman's voice probably sounded high and thin most of the time, but stress made it shrill. "They were in a box that we brought to the side of the dais right after the room opened. And now they're not there. We have no idea what happened to them."

"They're gone?" Scott asked. "And no one saw the box being moved?"

"No one. They're gone. But whoever took them left a note." Janelle held up a piece of paper.

In small block letters, written in pencil, it said, "Want to play a game? Appropriate for a toy show, don't you think? You want to find your trophies? Look where the big boys go."

"A treasure hunt?" Scott said, dumbfounded. "Someone wants to do a treasure hunt here?"

"Apparently," Janelle said. "And we don't have much choice. Or time."

"We're supposed to give them out right after dinner," Ms. Webster squeaked. "It's going to be so embarrassing if we can't."

"Let's get on it," Scott said. "The good news is whoever it was couldn't take them far. So where do the big boys go?"

"Bar? Sports bar?" I offered.

"I'm thinking more basic than that," Scott said. He looked around and spotted a men's rest room across the lobby.

Gilmont nodded. "You check in there. I'll find out if there are any others nearby."

Both men departed. I asked Ms. Webster, "How could someone take the awards without you seeing it? Isn't the box heavy?"

"The box was on a rolling cart. It happened after there was a commotion in the kitchen. Something got knocked over and we all went to check it out and make sure no one was hurt. When we came back, the cart was gone. It moved quietly, so it would be easy to take it while our backs were turned."

"That's consistent," I said. "This guy does distraction really well."

Gilmont had talked to someone at the concierge desk and walked off in the other direction. Moments later, Scott returned. He wasn't pulling a cart, but he had another piece of paper in his hands.

"Our thief has a twisted sense of humor," Scott said. "I found this taped to a mirror in the men's room." He passed it over to Janelle, who read:

"Knock, knock.

Who's there?

First.

First who?

First you have to thaw it out."

"Thinks he's a comedian." Gilmont had joined us and listened to Janelle read the note. "I suppose we're looking for a freezer. There's got to be another way to the kitchen without going through the banquet hall."

"I'll ask this time," Scott said. "I may have to tell them I'm event security."

Gilmont barely looked up from his study of the writing. "Go for it."

Scott returned a couple of minutes later. "Down the hall to the right. First left and the door marked 'Employees Only'."

We headed that way, found the door, and piled through, into a noisy, bustling space full of long tables, racks, ovens, and people. The aroma of warm bread mingled with that of sizzling beef, tangy sauce, and chocolate. The aroma reminded me of my brief foray into waitressing one summer after my freshman year in college. Those weren't fond memories, and this was no time to indulge them.

A large man in a white coat and hat approached us. His expression suggested a firecracker ready to blow. But he also held up a piece of paper and waved it at us. "I'm trying to manage an event and strangers keep rushing in and disturbing the work. As if I don't have problems enough already? Half of the chocolate cups fell apart. Some of the salmon wasn't fresh. The green beans…" He stopped, overcome by whatever problem the green beans presented. After a moment he shook the paper again. "You are looking for this? Some creature raced through earlier and slapped it on the freezer door."

"Did anyone get a good look at him?" Scott asked.

"I don't think so. He moved in and out like lightning. And he had this thing with a hood hiding his face."

"He wore dress pants and nice shoes," a young woman piped up from nearby. "I thought it was bizarre with the hoodie. He kept his head down and face hidden."

"Thank you," Scott said.

When Gilmont reached for the paper, the man pulled it back. "Who are you?"

"Detective Peter Gilmont, Metro Police. I don't have time to explain, but I need that paper. Call me Monday and I'll tell you about it." He pulled out a card and offered it.

The man turned over the paper in exchange and we headed back to the quiet hallway outside the kitchen to read it.

The sheet just said, "Nice work. Sorry I don't have time for more." But it had a second, smaller bit of paper attached—a claim ticket from the bell stand.

Ms. Webster's phone buzzed, not for the first time in the last few minutes, but this time she answered. "Yes," she said. "I know. I think we're about to get them. Just hold on for a few more minutes. Right." She ended the call and said, "They're about to start dessert service." Her voice got squeakier with each word and shook on the last few. "We're supposed to start once everyone has dessert and coffee."

"We'll have them shortly," Janelle said, trying to calm her. "There's still time."

I'd read about the action but have never actually seen someone wring their hands. MaryAnn Webster did just that. Her fingers twined around each other and squeezed as we strode quickly to the lobby again and crossed to the bell stand.

Gilmont gave the ticket to the man there, who disappeared into a small room behind the stand. Moments later he reappeared with a wheeled cart bearing a large box. The detective stopped before he reached us and lifted the lid, pulled out a couple of things, and looked around inside the box before setting the top down again. "I don't see any booby traps in there." He pushed it toward us.

"Oh, thank goodness," Ms. Webster said. She took the handle and started off across the lobby but paused after a few steps and turned toward us. "Thank you so much. I had no idea where to begin."

"And I have no idea what we might've missed while we've been playing this stupid game," Scott said.

Gilmont was looking at his phone and texting. "No re-

ports of anything unusual happening in the dining room."
He tucked the phone away in a pocket. "I want to go see
for myself."

"He had a reason for that game," Scott said before Gilmont left. "He wanted us out of the way while he did something. I wish I knew what."

"So do I," I added. "I'm at a loss."

We followed Janelle and Gilmont back to the ballroom,
but before we got to the door, Scott's phone buzzed. He
looked at it, backed away from the door, and put the device
to his ear. "Greg? What's up?" he asked. He listened for a
moment, then asked, "You're sure?" Another quiet space.
"Okay. On the way. Text with updates. I'm silencing my
phone."

He ended the call and turned to me. "Greg thinks there
might be something odd happening on the show floor."

TWENTY-TWO

Saturday

"ODD? LIKE WHAT?" I asked.

"Someone moving around," Scott answered. "Possibly not part of the cleaning crew. I'm letting Janelle know." He began tapping the small phone keyboard.

"How does he know it's not one of the cleaning people?"

Scott looked up from his phone. "He doesn't for sure. But one person doesn't seem to be in sync with the others. Doesn't appear to be mopping or vacuuming."

"What is he doing?"

"Not sure."

Janelle and Detective Gilmont emerged from the ballroom again and Scott explained.

Gilmont frowned. "Given the guy's MO, we can't dismiss it entirely. But we can't leave the dinner unprotected either. Just a minute."

He rushed back into the ballroom and was gone for a few moments before returning with two of the steely-faced men and one woman in tow. "Take them with you and head over to the Center."

"You have your key?" Janelle asked.

"I do," I said.

Scott stared at me, and I saw it in his expression before he spoke. "I'd prefer you stay here."

"Noted." I stared back at him. "But not happening."

He grimaced. "Okay. Try to stay behind me."

I agreed I could do that. Try, at least.

With the small security team, we rushed out of the hotel and across the street. Scott led us to a side door and stopped. He spoke to the group in a low tone, just above a whisper. "We don't know much about what's going on in there. Maybe nothing out of the ordinary. We know there's a cleaning crew working. It's possible that there is also someone else, maybe dressed in work clothes, pretending to be one of them. I know it's not much help. Just stay quiet and unobtrusively look for someone on his own who doesn't appear to be cleaning. We'll spread out once we're inside." He assigned a set of aisles to each person, and I explained where they were in relation to the entrance we'd be using. When I finished, Scott said, "Questions?"

"What do we do if spot a suspicious person?" the taller man asked.

"Follow, if you can without being seen, and text me for instructions." He asked each of the security guards to enter their numbers into his phone, while he put his in theirs.

He checked his phone for messages and said, "Change of plan. The possible suspect is currently moving up the nine hundred aisle. Detain if you can." He assigned two of the people to go up twelve hundred to the middle and one to cover seven hundred. We'd head directly for nine hundred.

I quietly unlocked a side door and shut off the alarm until everyone was inside. I had to take off my shoes to keep them from clacking on the stairs as we climbed up to the show floor level. Since we approached the hall from the back, I carefully opened one of the doors that said "Staff Only" on the other side, pulling gently to ensure it didn't squeak or rattle.

Inside I heard the distant creaking of a cart, probably one of the cleaning crew's, along with muffled voices. No sound of movement nearby, though. The huge overhead banks of fluorescents were off, but the emergency lights provided enough dim glow to let us see where we were going. In that half-light, the booths formed odd cityscapes with occasional looming towers and the lower copings of tables and bins lining the avenue of the aisle.

The other three people slipped off noiselessly to their assigned aisles, while I followed behind Scott to the end of nine hundred. We froze there when the squeak of a shoe sounded. It wasn't far from us, but not on this aisle. Scott consulted his phone and scanned a couple of messages. He jerked his head to the left, indicating we needed to head to the one thousand booths.

We quietly retreated and turned. Scott started up the aisle, stopped, and backed away. I had to step back quickly to avoid him, but I peered around and saw why he'd paused. A bit more than halfway between our position and the center aisle, a dark figure faced away from us. He stood by a bulky fixture in front of one of the booths, a series of wooden bins. A tarp had been thrown over it for the evening and the figure was lifting a corner to peer under the cover.

Scott texted the others on the team, giving them a few minutes to move closer before we approached. I watched the shadowy figure reach into the bin, move his arm around as though searching for something, and withdraw it. I was reminded of the gun found in the bin on the first day of the show. These weren't the same bins, or even the same company, but perhaps more than one had been planted. If he was retrieving a weapon, this could get ugly and dangerous quickly.

But he didn't appear to be holding anything when he

withdrew. I was pretty sure the figure was a man, though I couldn't say exactly why. Something about the slim build and shoulders looked masculine. A hooded sweatshirt kept his face in shadow.

He froze for a moment and looked up to see one of the security people appear in the center aisle. When he turned toward us and saw Scott at the other end, he elected not to run either way. Instead he dashed into the booth and slipped behind the backdrop. A crash from that direction suggested he'd met a barrier of some kind and pushed through it.

Scott made a hand motion, signaling to the other security people the direction the intruder had gone. We rushed to the next aisle and got there in time to see him scoot across and through another booth, leaving a spinner rack overturned in his wake. By the time we reached the eleven hundred aisle he was already well along it, nearing the center and watching for people approaching. I think he must've heard something. He ducked into the last booth on my side of the aisle and knocked over a stack of boxes so that it partly blocked the center walkway. One of those boxes contained a collection of loose balls. In the dim light I could barely make out several soccer-sized balls rolling down the aisle toward us.

Our quarry forced his way through the back of the booth.

We rushed to the next aisle, twelve hundred. Two of the other security people were visible again at the far end of the aisle. They'd made their way around the sprawled boxes and rolling balls, prepared to close in on him.

A strange set of noises clacked in the mostly hushed hall. I looked down to see moving shapes chugging up and down the aisle. It took a critical moment to recognize a squadron of toy cars and trucks deployed as distraction. They worked as obstructions as well.

Our quarry turned and moved toward us, then zigged

sharply to the right, through one of the larger booths that spanned both rows. The two guards at the far end came towards us, but they had to weave around the toy vehicles. One nearly tripped.

The man we pursued yanked at a loose tarp and tossed it over a series of display pods, blocking our view of him for a few seconds. When we caught sight of him again, he ran out of the far side of the booth and across the aisle, angled toward the center, and into one of the largest of the booths beyond, shoving over display racks and piles of merchandise as he went. He popped out the other side, building his lead on us.

I hoped the rest of the security people had heard the commotion and realized the quarry had doubled back. But I didn't see any of them at the center of the aisle he now traveled.

He didn't look back but must have heard us pursuing, since we'd given up on silence. As I raced after Scott, any fear I had dissolved in a wave of absolute rage. The guy, whoever he was, was making fools of us, in his warped pursuit of some unfathomable goal. I was tired of it. I was so over the theatrics, the drama, the destruction, the idiocy. Somewhere in my own anger, I got a glimpse of a motive. Not a rational, logical sort of glimpse, but a hint at the feeling, the emotion driving the destruction. And with that came a clue as to who the fleeing figure in the hoodie might be.

But we had to catch him because I couldn't think of any way to prove the connection. I didn't see anyone else as we followed him through yet another booth and watched him disappear behind the backdrop on the far side of the aisle. We hesitated, considering what to do next.

Scott pointed for me to return to the back end of the aisle

while he went up to the center. We both circled the row and I saw Scott in the middle when I got around. I didn't see any sign of the man we pursued, but a clatter and thunk made me think he was still somewhere in the booths on my right.

He burst out abruptly, closer to Scott's position than mine, and raced across again. The booth he entered had rows of shelves built at the back, blocking his way, but the next one had the usual tall, free-standing back display and he disappeared behind it. I went around to the next aisle and saw him come through the back of a booth closer to me.

I moved forward, hoping to distract him while Scott approached from the other direction. The other security people appeared behind Scott. Our quarry looked at them, then at me, and made up his mind. He charged. Straight toward me.

I'm embarrassed to admit I froze, shocked, and unable to decide what to do. I like to think I was trying to stop him by simply blocking the way, but it's not true. And in any case, it didn't work. Not totally anyway.

At the last minute, he veered around me, putting a hand on my arm and shoving me to the side. I went down, but as I did so, I stuck out a leg, and by sheer, lucky accident, managed to trip him. At the same time, I grabbed an object that rolled off a nearby display, hoping for something I could use as a weapon. Unfortunately, what I held was a soft foam miniature football. I threw it at him anyway.

It didn't slow him. He stumbled over my leg but didn't go down. He caught the football in one hand, on the move, and tossed it back at me before racing around the end of the aisle, turning to the left as he got there.

I fell into a rack holding sales sheets and brochures and ended up on my side with a blizzard of paper drifting around me. Scott and the others rushed past. Scott made a move toward me, but I shook my head. "I'm fine. Go after him."

I scrambled to my feet and raced right behind them as fast as I could. Two of the security people turned and went the other way, in an effort to double back and contain him. Scott and one of the security people were about ten feet ahead of me.

The quarry suddenly ducked into a booth on his right, and I swore under my breath when I recognized it. Play-Blox. I'd already guessed what he planned when he bent and flipped over the first one, then the second and third bins containing the mounds of plastic pieces the company left out to entice visitors to explore their creativity. He pushed the fourth and final bin in the other direction.

The resulting crash and scattering of blocks sounded like an avalanche in the formerly quiet hall. The bins smacked the floor with ear-splitting bangs while the scattering pieces rolled across the aisle in a clattering wave. I cursed even more, though not out loud, as I realized we'd all have to make our way across the uneven scree of plastic cubes and tubes to follow him. And I'd left my shoes back by the stairs.

Scott and the stocky security guy with him waded into the sea of blocks. Both struggled to keep their balance while crossing the shifting piles of rolling, crunching building toys. I was so not doing that. I stayed just long enough to see the man we pursued reach the center aisle and turn to his right. I ducked back to the end of the aisle and turned in the same direction he had.

When I got to the next row, I didn't see anyone at the far end, but I ran up it to the center aisle. There he was, off to my right now. Scott and his companion reached the center aisle just as I did. The other two security people were ahead of me, closer to him.

As I thought they were about to overtake him, the shadow figure turned and held something out toward his two pursuers. My stomach twisted in sudden, lurching fear that he might have a gun. The shape didn't look right, more like a can maybe, but from this distance I couldn't tell for sure. I dreaded the explosion when he fired.

He pressed a trigger at the top, but that didn't result in a gunshot. A strange hissing, swishing noise sounded instead. A long curl of something shot out of the can, twisting in the air in front of him, projecting eight feet or so between him and the two pursuing guards. It was followed by several more long, thin strings of...some kind of goo.

The thin, ropy stuff reached the guards and some of it clung to their faces and tangled in their hair. I let out the breath I'd been holding when I realized he'd fired a can of spray string. The can clattered when he tossed it aside, but it had done the job. Both agents were distracted, tangled in the goo and trying to keep the stuff from getting in their eyes and mouths, so they were late to take off after him when he ran.

He veered to his left up the six hundred aisle toward the front of the building. No doubt, he heard us pursuing, but he also now heard the clunk and woosh of a vacuum cleaner not far away and saw an escape route through the midst of the cleaners. He wasn't wrong, unfortunately.

He didn't veer off into any of the booths this time, but kept going until he reached the front aisle, where he turned to the right again, still heading for the sounds of the cleaning crew. The first of those in view, a man with a bucket and mop, looked up in alarm at the sight of a group of people running his way. He said something, pointing to the floor, but the words were indecipherable.

The cleaning man and his equipment blocked the passage, but our quarry didn't even slow down. The cleaner, frozen in either shock or indecision, didn't move as the vandal approached, veered around him, and shoved.

The cleaner fell to the side and the fleeing man rushed past him, heading for a door at the end of the exhibit hall. The corridor beyond it led to a staircase going down to a ground level exit, the one the cleaning crew used to get in and out. Neither Scott nor the others stopped to help the downed mop-wielder, but they were careful to jump over or go around him. It cost them a few decisive seconds.

The intruder pushed through the door, letting it bang shut behind him, and I could hear the tapping of his shoes on the stairs as he raced down. Scott and company weren't far behind, but I suspected the vandal would be outside before they could catch him. There were more than enough places out there where someone could disappear quickly in the darkness.

Several more cleaners had gathered around the downed man and helped him up. They chattered among themselves in another language. I followed the chasers to the door and through it, but I met Scott coming back up the stairs.

"He got out ahead of us," he said, sounding dejected. "The others are looking for him, but I doubt they'll have much success."

I drew a deep breath as the adrenaline surge of the chase began to wear off. "And now we have a lot more vandalism to explain to our exhibitors."

Scott gave me an odd look.

"What?" I asked.

He just shook his head. "Are you okay?"

I was starting to feel some bruises from the tumble I'd taken earlier, but nothing serious. "Fine. Except disappointed, furious, honked off, angry, enraged, and otherwise irritated."

A hint of a grin crossed his face. "Likewise."

I pulled in another deep breath and let it out slowly. "What do we do now?"

"I'm waiting for the rest of the—" A buzz from his phone interrupted him. "That's them now. No luck. I need to go let them in. The door to the outside locked behind them."

While Scott went to get his cohorts, I looked for the chief of the cleaning crew. The first person I asked gave me an uncomprehending stare, but the second pointed to a broad, short man talking with the mop-man who'd been bowled over.

He watched me approach with a disapproving expression that faded when I told him who I was and why we were there. He couldn't tell me much about the intruder, unfortunately. He'd noticed him, but didn't look closely, and couldn't describe him except to say that he'd had on nice shoes. Dress shoes, apparently. And maybe dress pants.

He hadn't seen the man's face.

I explained about the damage that had been done and asked them to fix anything they could. I promised a nice bonus for the crew in thanks.

Scott returned with the other security people, and we spent some time debating the next move. Two of them still had bits of spray string in their hair.

"He isn't likely to come back," I said. "Now he knows someone is watching. Also, the cleaning crew chief will notify me if they see him again." I rubbed a sore spot on my hip. "He'll probably go back to the banquet like nothing happened. Or just back to his hotel room. That would make more sense."

Scott's glance sharpened on me. "You know who it is?"

"I think so. But I was hoping we could catch him in here, because I don't know how else we can prove it."

"Tell me."

So I did.

TWENTY-THREE

Saturday-Sunday

BY THE TIME we returned to the ballroom, the awards presentation had ended. A band played and a few couples danced, but most of the crowd was settling in for social time or dispersing. We checked in with Janelle and Gilmont, who still circulated, watching the room.

I let Scott relate what had happened on the show floor. I looked around but didn't see any of the parties from Donneywell, Carrie Classics, GlamourThings, Handley, or even the ones I knew from Juvenile Retail News, until I noticed Daryl Hilderman interviewing Olivia Donneywell. Since she held a plaque, I assumed their dragons had won one of the awards.

Scott mentioned I had suspicions about the identity of the vandal but no actual evidence to back them up. Gilmont listened to my reasons, but didn't commit to anything other than to say, "It might be a good idea to keep a watch on the booth tomorrow. I'm still trying to figure out who killed Lorene Donneywell. It may be connected but I'm not convinced."

I felt the same.

At eleven, we agreed any further incidents were unlikely and headed for home. Tomorrow would be another workday. The last day of the show and our last chance to catch the vandal and solve a murder. That wasn't too much to accomplish.

To GIVE ME maximum time for sleep, Scott picked me up the next morning instead of my taking the Metro downtown. Not much traffic impeded us on Sunday morning.

Scott planned to spend much of the day watching for our vandal, keeping tabs on my suspect in hopes of catching him in the act. I thought it unlikely he'd do anything now, but since none of the vandalism had been particularly rational, maybe whatever urge pushed him into it would drive him to another attempt.

In the meantime, I'd have to determine how much of last night's destruction had been repaired and be prepared to deal with some angry exhibitors. We stopped for much-needed coffee at a drive-through. The jolt of caffeine chased away the drowsiness from the too-short night's sleep but did little to improve my mood.

Janelle was already in her office, going over a list with Gilmont, when we arrived. They looked up as I tapped on the door. Both had shadows under their eyes and drawn expressions.

"Any new developments I should know about?" I asked.

Janelle picked up her pen and twirled it. "Don't we wish."

"What I expected."

Scott told them his plans.

Janelle said, "Sounds good."

I checked my phone. "Show floor opens to exhibitors in three minutes. I'd better head down there. I expect complaints."

Gilmont stood. "I need to talk to a few people about a murder."

The three of us went downstairs in grim silence. I planned to retrace the vandal's route as best I could, making sure any damage had been repaired and calm any irritated exhibitors. As we headed on to the show floor, my companions went their separate ways while I found the place where we'd first spotted the intruder the previous evening.

The booth looked far more colorful and lively this morning in the bright light and with its displays uncovered. I considered the bin the intruder had reached into, and an idea burst in my brain. His hand had come out empty and that didn't seem to surprise him. What if he'd been putting something into it rather than trying to retrieve an object? Now that I thought about it, there might've been something in his hand when he reached in.

Cold washed over me and odd, wavy, colored lines crossed my vision for a moment. Breath caught in my throat as I considered the possibilities. Heartbeat sped up.

The bin held an assortment of brightly colored stuffed bears. The basic design was the same for all the animals, but their bodies, heads, muzzles, and other parts shone with an assortment of saturated reds, oranges, blues, yellows, and greens.

A man approached and said, "The bears are keyed to various aspects of a child's personality. The colors are—"

I held up a hand to halt the sales pitch, identified myself, and explained what had happened the previous evening. No one on their staff had noticed anything amiss when they uncovered the bins, and Don Albertson didn't look happy when I asked to take the animals out of the section on the far left.

They agreed only because no customers roamed the area at the time. Two of the young sales associates helped pull fuzzy animals out of the bin, until one held up an object that looked nothing like a bear and said, "What the heck is this?"

She raised a cylinder about four or five inches long and two inches in diameter. A colorful red label on it read "Smoke Show." Attached to the side, a coin-shaped metal object had six boxes showing digital numbers. The two at the far right changed rapidly, appearing to count down. Each time they reached zero, the third from the right notched down one. A timer. It appeared set to do something in an hour and twenty-two minutes.

I didn't want to say aloud what I thought it was, and fortunately I didn't need to. One of the other people in the booth recognized the cylinder. "Smoke bomb," he said. Seeing our reaction, he held up a hand. "Wait, no, don't panic. It's not that kind of bomb."

The man, whose tag identified him as Cam Holton, looked more closely. "Yeah, it's the kind of thing they use for parties and plays when they need smoke. We used them at the gender reveal party for my daughter a few years ago."

"So they're not dangerous?" I asked.

"I don't know. They do explode out of the can, and I think there's some heat when they do. Plus, they'd probably startle people. Maybe cause a panic?" He looked at the can and the bin again. "Would've made a heck of a mess if it had gone off in there. They blow out a bunch of colored powder."

I got on the phone to Scott and asked him to join me. This was becoming a bad habit. Fortunately, he was nearby. The crowd remained sparse this early on a Sunday morning, so he arrived within minutes. It took a couple more to fill him in.

His brow wrinkled and mouth pulled into a frown as he looked at the canister, then softened into a tight smile.

"Party popper," he said. "Safe enough when used properly, but not meant for indoors."

"On a timer, set to go off in an hour and fourteen minutes now. Put here last night. What if there are others?" I asked. "He had about fifteen minutes before we got here."

His grin disappeared. I didn't need to spell out the potential complications. Scott got on the phone to his friend Greg, apologized for waking him up early after a late night, quickly explained our problem, and asked if he would review the video to see if the intruder had planted other smoke bombs. He added that if all the timers were set the same way, we had an hour and twelve minutes to find them.

While we waited for Greg to call back, Scott asked for a bag. The young woman who'd found the smoke bomb went off to get one. Scott and Cam Holton examined the device and discussed removing the timer. They finally agreed that if they taped the pin in place, they could remove the electronic countdown clock. Holton found Scotch tape, and they gingerly removed the timer without the thing going off. The woman returned with a bag and Scott dropped both pieces in.

Meanwhile I called Janelle and filled her in. I had to rush to update her on our plan to find any others. "He couldn't have planted too many," I speculated. "There wasn't that much time."

"Hope so. We may have to make a general announcement."

"Ouch. I hope not. That would risk causing panic."

"I know," she said. "I want to avoid that. But if you're not reasonably sure you have them all with fifteen minutes to go, I want to know about it."

Scott's phone buzzed and I told Janelle I had to go. He listened for a moment, then said, "Got it. Just stay on the line with me and keep looking." He turned to me. "Seventeen hundred aisle, fourth booth from the back on the left."

"Good luck," the man who'd identified the smoke bomb called as we raced off.

With Greg on the line, we verified we were at the right booth as we arrived. The company sold baby dolls in assorted sizes.

"Behind a stack of boxes on the right," Scott relayed.

The stack in question was a six-foot-tall pyramid of packaged, standing dolls. The front of the boxes all had clear plastic windows, so dozens of faces peered out at us from that tower. I spotted where one of the lower containers wasn't lined up straight and moved it aside carefully, fearful of bringing down the entire tower.

Scott handed me a pair of latex gloves. "Use these. I can't operate the phone with gloves on," he said, when I raised an eyebrow.

A woman spotted us and approached from the back of the booth like an armed tank, ready to do battle. I let Scott explain while I reached into the crevice left when I moved the box and felt around the floor inside the stack. It took only moments to locate and pull out a cylinder like the other one. The color of the label differed, but it had a similar device attached. Comparing the two showed they were set to go off at the same time, and we now had fifty-three minutes to find any others. Scott held the bag open, while apologizing to the woman in charge. I dropped the cylinder in. He put his phone to his ear and said, "We found it."

After listening for a moment, Scott said, "Got the next one." I hurriedly added my apologies to the woman and promised explanations would be forthcoming but would have to wait.

"Fourteen hundred, near the front, six booths from the center aisle, on the right.

"Behind the backdrop," Scott added as we rushed that way. "Left side as we approach. You go straight for it. I'll handle explanations."

The booth in question featured a variety of outdoor toys including water slides, pools, water guns and balloons, and soaker rifles and cannons. Built into the backdrop, a huge digital screen showed videos of children playing with their products.

Per the plan, I ignored everyone in the booth and headed straight for the side of the massive display unit. Not surprisingly several boxes stowed behind it held pamphlets, sell sheets, and order forms. Good thing we were near the end of the show. They'd probably started with a lot more boxes than these, but I still had to dig around in two of them before I found it, wedged down in a corner.

"Got it." I brought it to Scott and dropped it in the bag. We were down to thirty-six minutes. Again, we offered our apologies and promised explanations later before heading off.

My phone buzzed while we waited for Greg to find the next target. I checked, thinking it might be Janelle, but it was a ping from the GlamourThings booth. I quickly texted that I'd check in with them later.

Scott nodded sharply and said, "Twelve hundred. On the corner at the center aisle. Right side."

We rushed to the booth, which was another purveyor of stuffed animals. These were small and sold in sets, however. The booth was enclosed on two sides by walls made of stacks of boxes with pyramids of them at the edges.

"Help," I said, surveying the extent of the possibilities.

"Greg's not sure. Right side, toward the back. He thinks."

A man approached with a smile and greeting, but I ignored both to see if I could peer around behind the walls of boxes. Unfortunately, since the booth was on a corner, the right side also opened to the center aisle and the wall had been built in two layers, one with the boxes facing the inside of the booth and the other oriented toward the center aisle. There appeared to be a narrow space between them, but it was too dark to let me see in there. No out-of-place package helped me figure out where it might be.

I jerked out my phone and fumbled for the flashlight app. My shaking hands meant it took longer than it should have before I got the light on. I ran the beam along the narrow crevice for several feet before I spotted it.

"I see it," I told Scott. But the thing was at least a foot beyond my reach, which meant I'd have to remove a box from the wall. Unlike the pyramids of earlier, which were relatively stable, I feared that removing any single unit could collapse a good part of the structure.

Scott looked to the man who'd approached and stood watching us. "There's something we need to retrieve behind those boxes," he explained. "We don't want to risk knocking it over, but I'm afraid we have to."

The man, bless him, didn't argue. Instead, he suggested, "If you and I hold the boxes in place on either side, while she moves one, I think we can manage to keep it up."

I measured the distance with my eye and went to the spot in the wall I hoped was close to where the cylinder lay. I pushed a package on the bottom row. Scott and the other man flanked me on the wall, bracing the stacks with their entire bodies while I gingerly nudged a package backward on one side. As I'd hoped, it rotated instead of sliding straight back, leaving a narrow space but keeping enough of its bulk in place to support the weight above it.

I reached into the opening and groped. It took a few precious moments to find the cylinder, grab it, and pull it out. Eighteen minutes left, according to the display. We took the timer off it and dropped it in the bag. I let out a deep breath and sagged in relief.

Scott talked into the phone again before saying to me, "Greg's pretty sure that's all of them. He's checking the tape again to be sure, but his next stop was where we first saw him last night."

"He meant to do more of them. What about the others? Did he already have them all set to go?"

Scott's eyes widened and he spoke into the phone. "Can you tell if he set the timers on them before he put each one in?"

Scott switched the phone to speaker, so I could hear when Greg answered. "It looks like he does do something to them before dropping them in place."

I let out a long breath. "I hope that's got them. We could have quite a show otherwise."

Scott nodded. I helped him remove the timers from the other cylinders, then called Janelle and told her I thought we had them all.

"How confident are you?" she asked.

I considered. "Eighty to ninety percent."

"Good enough. I'm coming down right now, just in case."

We picked a spot near the center of the floor to wait out the countdown. Janelle joined us with the timer reading just two minutes remaining. We showed her the objects we'd gathered.

"Those would've made quite the mess," she said dryly.

"Will, if we missed any," I agreed. "But…" I ruminated out loud. "Another diversion?"

"From what?" Scott asked. "This seems more like a

statement." He suddenly turned and said, "I want to observe your suspect when nothing happens. We hope."

Janelle and I followed. I held one of the disabled timers and watched it count down seconds as it got to under a minute. We stationed ourselves a couple of booths down and waited.

The person I suspected was engaged with a couple of potential customers and showed no sign of anticipation.

The timer ticked off the last few seconds and I felt the little arm on the mechanism release with a tiny ping. Had it still been connected to the cylinder that would have set it off.

I listened intently. Nothing out of the ordinary reached me from any direction. Just the sounds of business carrying on. I waited, hardly daring to believe we had, in fact, succeeded. After a couple of minutes, I unclenched my fists and looked at Janelle.

"I think we dodged that bullet," I said. I watched the suspect carry on as normal. "But it doesn't help us prove anything, either."

Janelle gave me a crooked grin. "I'd still rather have the crisis averted. Even if it does cost us a way to prove a suspicion. I'll head back upstairs now."

My stomach slowly untwisted itself. I couldn't decide how I felt. Relieved, certainly, but also concerned, and even a bit flat. The adrenaline surge of the search and retrieve mission waned, leaving a strange emptiness in its place.

My phone buzzed again, and I answered without thinking.

"Miss McNeil? It's Emilia Grinkoff. At GlamourThings? My brother has something he wants to tell you. It's important."

TWENTY-FOUR

Sunday

I THOUGHT OF all the upset people we'd just left in the wake of our search for the smoke bombs, and the ones whose booths had been disrupted the previous evening during the chase. I wondered how important whatever Josef had to say could truly be.

"I'll be there in a couple of minutes," I told her.

I think I agreed to see her mostly to put off having to deal with all those aggrieved exhibitors.

At the GlamourThings booth, I found Emilia Grinkoff talking to a neighboring exhibitor while Josef perched on a stool in a corner, drawing on a sketch pad that sat on his lap. He saw me first. His expression broke into a wide grin, and he hopped up.

He tapped his sister's shoulder and pointed to me when she turned to him. They both came over.

"Miss McNeil." Emilia gave me a strange, narrow-eyed smile. "I'm still annoyed about the booth change, but you've been kind to Josef, so I owe you for that. He has something he needs to show you. I don't quite understand what he's talking about, so maybe we could borrow the young lady who does sign language?"

"She does need to work," I said. "Unless it's really important, I hate to disturb her again."

Josef tapped my arm gently and picked up his sketch-book. He lifted a couple of sheets to show me a well-executed charcoal drawing of a man wearing a hoodie. I stared at it, trying to decipher what I was seeing. The hoodie obscured the man's eyes and upper face, but the nose and jawline were familiar.

It reminded me...

I needed Terry. "I'll be right back."

Fortunately, the young woman wasn't engaged with a customer when I got to the booth where she worked. "Can I borrow you for a moment?" I asked her.

She looked at another, older woman, her boss, I pre-sumed. I glanced at the other woman, too, and introduced myself. "I need Terry for a couple of minutes," I added. "Shouldn't be long, but it's a public service. She's helping me communicate with a deaf exhibitor."

The older woman hesitated before saying, "Why not? It's quiet for the moment, anyway."

I thanked her and we walked to GlamourThings. "I think Josef knows something very important about a major prob-lem we've had," I told Terry on the way.

She and Josef greeted each other with smiles and a series of hand gestures. Then he pointed to the picture, and they discussed it for a few minutes. Terry's eyes grew wider, and she looked both surprised and concerned. She turned to me once Josef stopped.

"He says this is a sketch he drew of a man he saw last night. He thinks you were there, at the awards ceremony. He said this man tried to steal the awards. Is that possible?"

"Not just possible. It happened. And this is the guy who did it?"

"Josef doesn't know who it is, but he hoped his sketch would help you identify the person."

"Jiminy Christmas." I grabbed my phone and punched the icon for Scott. "We've got him. An eyewitness saw him stealing the awards last night. He drew a picture. The top of the head is hidden by the hoodie, but the mouth and jaw are clear. It's him."

"Okay. I'm watching him," Scott said. "Haven't seen any reaction to the smoke bombs not going off. How do you want to handle it?"

"I think we need Gilmont and Janelle to decide that. I'll give her a buzz."

"I'll wait," he said.

I turned to Terry again. "Can you tell him this could be very helpful indeed. We know who this person is but haven't been able to connect him definitely to the various incidents until now. We may need Josef to talk to the director and the police. Would he do that?"

She translated my words. Josef looked serious and reluctant, but after a moment, he nodded.

"Good." I smiled at him. "Tell him I need to discuss this with my boss before we do anything, but we'll talk to him more about it later."

While she did that, I buzzed Janelle and said, "Need to consult right now if possible. We might have him."

She didn't hesitate. "Come up to my office."

When I got there, she was tapping a pen against a piece of paper on her desk. The action was jerky and hurried. "Pete's on the way. I asked Scott to stay and keep an eye on your suspect."

Gilmont came in a moment later and we filled him in. "How sure is the identification?" he asked.

"Good enough, I'd say," I answered. "The man who drew the picture is talented, and I recognized the subject immediately even though the eyes were obscured."

The detective looked at Janelle. "You want to tackle him on the floor or try to lure him off somewhere? He'll likely figure out we're onto him and disappear."

"Scott's watching him. He can follow if he does run," I offered.

"I'd like to have more evidence to connect him to the vandalism," Gilmont said. "I'll see if we can get a warrant to search the booth and his hotel room." He spent a moment texting on his cell phone.

"Time isn't on our side," Janelle said. "This is our chance to get him. Ordinarily I'd be dead set against this, but I think we need to talk to him in the booth. No warning, no time for him to get away or dispose of any evidence."

"All right," Gilmont said. "Let's go. A confession would be the best possible outcome."

I texted Scott to let him know what we were about to do. He responded with one word. "Good."

"How do we approach this?" I asked on the way.

"Confidently," Gilmont suggested. "Convince him we have no doubt and he'll be better off confessing. Do we know why he did it? There's got to be something personal behind it, something bugging him."

"Screwed up family," I offered.

"There are way too many of those," he said. "But it's a pressure point. Let's work it."

My emotions churned as we got to the show floor. The triumph I'd felt earlier had faded into doubt and dread. This could get ugly.

My phone pinged with a text from Scott. "He just left the booth and is currently in a rest room on the southwest side."

I showed it to both Janelle and Gilmont.

"Let's grab him when he comes out," Janelle suggested.

I relayed that, even as I spotted Scott a couple of hundred feet down. He looked up, saw us, and indicated our quarry was still inside the men's room.

We joined him and waited while several other men emerged. Finally, he came out.

We moved in to surround him. Gilmont said, "Mr. Langley? Ross Langley? D.C. Police. We'd like to talk to you about some incidents that have happened here over the last few days."

The young man swiveled, looking for a way to run, but with the wall behind and the four of us in a circle around him, he had no place to go. Instead, he opted for ignorance.

"What's this all about? What are you talking about?"

He did aggrieved innocence well. But seeing him up close again, I was even more sure.

"Let's go somewhere more private," Gilmont suggested. We escorted him off the show floor, to a conference room nearby. Once in the hall, he swerved sharply left in a bid to escape, but Scott grabbed his arm after a couple of steps.

"Running doesn't help your claims of innocence," he remarked.

"I don't understand what's going on. Why're you kidnapping me?"

"We're not kidnapping you," Gilmont said. "We're escorting you to a quiet place to talk."

"Are you arresting me?"

"Not yet. Not unless I have to. It would be easier for all of us if you'd just come with us."

He sighed dramatically. "All right. Let's get this over with. I need to get back to the booth as soon as possible." He grabbed a bottle of water from a table we passed.

We let Gilmont do the talking after we settled in the conference room. "I'm not asking if you committed the acts of vandalism that have happened during this show. We know you did. I want to know why."

Ross gave us a blank look, casually opened the water bottle with a steady hand, and took a drink. "I have no idea what you're talking about." He looked around at each of us, finally settling his gaze on me. "Miss McNeil, I don't understand why you're part of this…farce."

"Because I know you're responsible."

He rolled his eyes and shook his head. "I've had enough. Either arrest me and show me whatever proof you think you have or let me go."

"We have a warrant to search your hotel room."

His grin had a nasty cast. "Good luck with that. We checked out this morning. Heading home tonight. My bag is stowed at the bell stand if you want to search it. I'll save you the trouble of getting a warrant. Go ahead."

So, he'd either disposed of the remaining smoke bombs and any other evidence, or he had them stashed somewhere else.

"We will," Gilmont promised.

Langley stood. "In the meantime, I have work to do. Unless you're going to arrest me now, I'm leaving."

Gilmont looked at each of us in turn. Scott gave a small shake of his head, and I did the same. None of us attempted to stop the young man as he stalked out of the conference room.

"What now?" Gilmont asked as the door closed behind him.

"Now we watch the booth," Scott said. "Without him seeing us. Heather and I both think he didn't plant all of his smoke bombs last night. And I have the feeling he's still going to try for one more big attack."

"Can you handle that?" Gilmont asked. "We haven't yet

tied him—or anyone else—to the Donneywell murder, and I still need to talk to some people about it."

Scott pulled a pair of rubber gloves from a belt pouch and put them on, then gathered up the bottle of water Langley had left on the table, holding it in two fingers around the bottom. He handed it to Janelle. "Take this upstairs and seal it in a paper bag. Write your name, date, and time across the seal. In case we need to match fingerprints or DNA."

He turned back to Gilmont. "I'm working with people at a booth across the aisle who'll let me hide behind a display to watch him. He won't know I'm there."

"And I've got a lot of apologies to make in a short time," I said. "Let me know if he makes a move."

We scattered to do our various jobs. I wasn't thrilled about mine, but I needed to make amends with as many exhibitors as I could.

Most of the people I talked with were gracious about the disruption we'd caused, especially those where they'd seen us remove one of the smoke bombs. Even the ones whose booths had been damaged the previous evening were generally nicer about it than I expected. Of course, rumors had been flying about the events of the night before, and they all wanted the latest update on the situation from me.

At quarter to one I got a text from Scott saying "He's leaving the booth, wearing baseball cap and coat. Got a bag. Going to intercept."

I made another hasty apology and left. I was only a couple of aisles down and arrived in time to see Scott standing in front of Langley, blocking his path. He could ask to look in the bag but couldn't legally demand it. Time for me to get clumsy.

I approached, trying to work out the best angle. The bag Langley carried over his right shoulder was a cheap tote with the Carrie Classics logo. Nothing held the top closed, which worked in my favor.

Another bit of luck came my way. When I stopped abruptly right beside Ross Langley, a startled and perhaps distracted gentleman behind me didn't get the message in time and careened into my back, knocking me off balance.

With just a bit of twisting redirection, I used the momentum to send myself crashing into Langley's side. The tangle of our bodies hid the motion when I hooked a finger in the strap of the tote and jerked. Even if he suspected my intent, the move could easily be seen as an attempt to grab hold of something to restore my balance.

Even more helpful, the gentleman behind extended a hand to steady me while apologizing profusely for his clumsiness. "That's fine," I tried to assure him. "Thanks for the assistance." In turn, I tried to apologize to Ross Langley. He ignored me. He'd just realized the contents of the tote bag had scattered, and Scott was now picking up one of the escaping smoke bombs.

He held it up just as Ross, myself, and the man who'd run into me untangled ourselves and found our balance again.

"Lose something, Langley?" he said.

I felt the young man's muscles tense and wrapped an arm around him. "No, you're not going anywhere," I said, hanging on as he tried to shake me loose and move away.

TWENTY-FIVE

Sunday

"THIS PROBABLY ISN'T the best place for this discussion," Scott said. "Back to the booth."

"That may not be the best place, either." I held onto Langley until Scott moved to his other side and clasped the other arm.

"I'm not chancing him wiggling away again."

Between the two of us, we nudged and shuffled Ross Langley back to the booth. Only one customer was there, talking to Sam Schultz and another young woman. Janice watched us approach and came over to ask, "What's going on?"

"You might want to ask Ross," I told her. "We all want to know why he was planting smoke bombs in other exhibitors' booths. With timers to set them off."

Janice looked irritated and perplexed. "What are you talking about?"

"Yeah, what are you talking about?" Ross taunted.

"These." Scott held two of them up and looked at Ross's mother. "Smoke bombs. Ask him why he had five of them in a tote bag and where he was taking them. I assume those are the five that didn't get planted last night." He held up several of the half-dollar-sized timers.

"This is crazy," Janice said. "There must be some mistake. Why would Ross do something like that?"

"That is the question, isn't it?" Scott said. "We'd all like to know the answer." He turned to Ross. "Since last night didn't go as planned, were you going for another display? Right before the end of the show?"

"No idea what you're talking about."

"Yet you were carrying a company-branded tote bag holding these." Scott held up one of the smoke bombs. "Last night you planted several of them in various booths around the hall, set to go off at ten o'clock this morning. It was quite a plan to disrupt the show. Too bad someone watched you, and we were able to collect them before they exploded."

Janice came closer and took one of the smoke bombs from Scott. "He really was carrying these? And he planted others last night?"

"Most definitely he was carrying them," I said, supporting Scott's accusation. "If the man behind me hadn't bumped into me and sent me into him, he probably would've taken them to set off somewhere. Was that Plan B?" I asked him. "Since last night's efforts failed?"

Ross gave me a hard, cold stare but didn't answer.

I directed my next question to his mother. "He came to the Awards Gala last night, but he didn't stay long, did he?"

"He was feeling off and went back to his room," the woman answered.

"Only he didn't go back to his room. He stole the awards from the dinner and hid them to create a diversion while he came over here, pretended to be part of the cleaning crew to get into the exhibit hall, and planted smoke bombs before we chased him off. And, yes, we can prove it."

Janice Langley's eyes widened as she looked at her son. "They can prove it?"

"They can't prove a thing."

"Oh, but we can. We have a witness who saw you steal the awards last night. We also have you on video pulling some of your pranks."

"Ross." Janice's tone was impatient and hard. Her eyes narrowed, mouth pulled tight. "Why?"

He turned a startled look on his mother. "You believe them. Them! Not me." His demeanor changed suddenly, alarmingly. The harsh reserve that sat oddly on his youthful features altered, replaced by a wide-eyed...wildness, was the only way I could describe it. His gaze shot rapidly around the area, mouth drooped, shoulders rounded forward, and a flush colored his cheeks. He vibrated with tension. "And that's the problem, isn't it?" He stared at his mother, aiming his words at her like darts. Or bullets. "Always someone or something else is more important to you than me." His voice rose louder and higher. Much louder. "I've never come first with you, have I? The job was more important. The clients were more important. The business took precedence. My whole life. This company, the business, this industry was always more important to you than I was."

The other people in the booth had stopped talking and turned to look. The shouting drew attention from others in surrounding booths and the aisles as well.

I looked at Scott and shook my head. I was starting to feel sorry for both Ross and his mother, but we needed to get this off the show floor. Scott must have texted for help at some point earlier. Two other show security people approached. We surrounded Ross as he kept shouting.

"This company. You'd do anything for it, wouldn't you?

You and him." He pointed to Sam Schmidt. "Sleep around, lie, bribe, cajole, pay hush money. Anything for the company. For success." Ross was quite literally raving now.

Janice's lips quivered and her eyes gleamed with tears. I glanced over at Schmidt and caught a flash of intense dismay, almost horror, on his face. Something clicked into place in my brain, but I didn't have time to follow it up right then.

Janice took her son's arm and put a finger over his lips. "Hush now. Please. Let's go someplace more private to talk." She turned toward Scott and me. "Is there someplace we can go?" she asked. "Someplace close, but private?" I nodded. Scott said, "Yes."

I led the way down the aisle toward the front, sidestepping to keep an eye on them. Ross let his mother guide him. He stopped shouting but something like convulsive sobs shook his body. Scott held his arm, and the two other security people got in place behind them. I texted Janelle as we headed for a conference room. Decisions would have to be made, but those were way above my pay grade. Thank goodness.

Besides, I needed to talk to Gilmont. Quickly.

Janelle met us as we got to the door. I let the others go in while I waited with her outside. Once the door shut behind them, I gave her a quick brief on what had happened. "Oh, man," she sighed. "What a way to end the show."

"Not over yet," I said. "I need to talk to Gilmont. Right now."

She texted him and waited for a response. "He's on the way. I told him it was an emergency."

"It is."

TWENTY-SIX

Sunday

IT TOOK GILMONT three long minutes to arrive. By then Janelle had gone into the conference room to figure out what to do about Ross Langley. I was ready to start chewing my nails.

I went to meet him when I saw the detective approaching, took his arm to turn him around, and said, "Please, come with me." I explained why as we hurried back to the show floor.

"You're sure about this?" he asked as we neared the booth.

"Not positive, but it all fits together."

He waited a moment before saying, "It's plausible."

We returned to the Carrie Classics display to find a subdued crew of two, the young woman I'd seen with Sam Schmidt, and a middle-aged man I sort of remembered noticing there before. Gilmont went up to the man and asked, "Is Sam Schmidt around?"

The man looked flustered and puzzled. "You saw what happened here earlier," he said to me. "Sam went to see what he could do to help."

"No, he didn't," I said.

"You're sure of that?" Gilmont asked.

"I waited outside the conference room for you. He had

plenty of time to get there if he'd followed us." I turned to the man whose name tag said he was Al Portman. "Does Mr. Schmidt have a car here?"

"Yeah. He and a couple others drove in."

"Do you know where it's parked?"

"Hotel parking deck, I imagine."

I led the way as we rushed down the escalator to the main entrance and out the door. The parking deck was on the other side of the hotel building from the main entrance right across the street. As we exited the Market Center, the glass doors into the lobby swung shut behind a figure that looked like Schmidt. Traffic was steady and we had to wait a couple of minutes for even a small break to let us cross.

Gilmont pulled out his phone while we waited and re-quested backup. I doubted any could arrive in time, but he also asked for someone to call the hotel right away and tell them to stop anyone from entering the parking deck for the next few minutes. I wasn't sure even that message could reach the right people before Schmidt made it there.

Finally, a traffic light changed, creating a small gap in the stream of vehicles. We raced across the street and into the front door of the hotel, along the lobby, and toward the door to the parking deck.

Two men stood at the door, one blocking the path of the other. Neither was Schmidt. "Been here long?" Gilmont asked the man doing the blocking. He wore a hotel uniform.

He shook his head. "Only a minute. Someone told me to get over here and keep anyone from leaving by this door."

"Did you see someone go through before you got here?"

He considered, but it was actually the other man, who wore a suit and toted a rolling suitcase, who answered. "I saw a man go out just before we got here. Older middle-aged maybe? Medium height. Bit overweight. Reddish complexion and silver hair."

"Sounds like him," I said.

Gilmont held up his badge for the hotel employee to see. "Have someone block the exit."

"There are two."

"Block them both. No one leaves." Gilmont tossed the words back as we rushed out the door to the parking deck. We stood on the second level. The elevator in the center showed the cab was on the fifth floor.

Gilmont stared at the display a moment, then grimaced. "The exits are our best bet." We chugged down the staircase next to the elevator well. His phone buzzed. "Good. Get a unit at each exit from the hotel parking garage. And another at the back exit from the hotel. I texted a description of the suspect."

We emerged on the ground level to the blare of honking horns from drivers already upset at the delay. Straight ahead of us a line of five or six cars waited at one of the exits. A police car with lights on blocked the narrow lane beyond the retractable gate. Another SUV drove up and joined the line as we watched.

Gilmont went to the nearest car and looked in, then went to the next. At the third one, tinted windows prevented him seeing the driver, so he tapped the window, while holding up his badge. A woman rolled down the window and asked, "What's going on?"

He didn't hang around to answer but raced to the next car in the line. Once he'd determined no one in this line was the man we sought, he signaled to the car blocking the exit to let the group he'd checked go.

We turned around and raced to the other side. As we approached the cars waiting there, the door of the fourth

in line opened and a silver-haired man jumped out. He
ran toward an unblocked pedestrian doorway. We chased
after him.

I didn't see what happened, and I'm glad I didn't. We
were still on the wrong side of the door to the street when
we heard the desperate squeal of brakes and raucous screech
of tires on pavement, followed by an ominous thunk.

Someone screamed as I followed Gilmont to the side-
walk outside the parking deck. The officer who'd been in
the car blocking the exit was already out and headed toward the street.

Sam Schmidt's body sprawled across the pavement ten
feet in front of us. In his desperation he must've run straight
out into the road where he'd been hit by the SUV that clearly
tried to stop in time but didn't have enough space.

Gilmont and the other officer approached to check on
him. Moments later, I knew Schmidt was dead.

All I could think about was the hideous irony that he
died in the same way as the woman he'd murdered.

TWENTY-SEVEN

Sunday

WE WERE AN exhausted foursome at the tapas restaurant that evening for a late dinner. The toy show had ended. Lots of rumors about Carrie Classics circulated for the rest of the afternoon, though few people knew all that happened.

Ross Langley had been taken to a local hospital and was being evaluated for admission to the Psych Ward. More consultation with the DA would be needed to decide what, if any charges, would be filed against him.

Gilmont's afternoon was filled with paperwork related to Sam Schmidt's death. I'd spent an hour with the near-hysterical woman who'd been driving the SUV that hit him. Gilmont and I had both assured her the accident was in no way her fault, since Schmidt had run right out in front of her. I guided the vehicle to a parking place at the curb while she called her husband, and I waited with her for him to arrive.

I'd spent the next half hour retelling the events to Janelle and Scott before finally returning to the show for its last hour. I was practically dizzy with relief that it was all over.

Once we'd ordered food, Gilmont said, "I just got confirmation from the police in Connecticut that a search of Schmidt's office turned up a blackmail note from Lorene

Donneywell in a locked drawer. She threatened to tell his stepfather they had an ongoing affair." He looked at me. "But you'd already figured that out. How?"

"I didn't know that's what she was holding over him. But I put together bits and pieces from various conversations with people who knew them both. Sam Schmidt's stepfather owned Carrie Classics and he'd threatened to cut Sam out when he'd raised the possibility of divorcing his wife before. Schmidt himself told me he'd had a brief affair with Lorene in the past, but others indicated there might have been more to it than that. Jessie said Lorene got a note from someone at Carrie Classics she didn't want anyone else to see and Lorene expected a cash infusion in the near future."

I stopped and waited while a server brought glasses of sangría for myself and Janelle. Scott and Gilmont, who'd be driving each of us home that night, opted for soft drinks. I took a long pull at the wonderful, peach-flavored drink before continuing. "The final piece, though, was when Ross was raving about all the bad things happening in the industry and he mentioned hush money. I happened to look at Schmidt right then and saw what looked like absolute horror on his face as he realized Ross knew about the blackmail. It freaked me out at the time, but we were so wrapped up in containing Ross I couldn't do anything about it right away."

Scott saluted me with his soda glass. "You also managed to identify Ross Langley as the likely vandal. What made you tag him for it?"

"A combination of the general build and his attitude. Plus, the hats."

"Hats?"

"When we saw him on the video in the cowboy hat, I was reminded of similar hats I'd seen before. But I didn't put it together until later. A few days ago—it seems like months ago now—in the Carrie Classics booth, they were doing this silly play to attract attention to their products, and some of the actors wore cowboy hats. Not the same hat, but it roused my suspicions. Then it occurred to me that the connection the vandalized exhibitors had with Lorene Donneywell would likely apply equally to Janice Langley, since they went after the same products. None of that would have been enough, though, without Josef Grinkoff's sketch of the man who stole the awards. I hope that's going to be helpful."

Gilmont nodded. "Very. Together with his statement about what he saw. Plus, whatever matches we can get from the water bottle, the drone, and the smoke bombs. We didn't find any acid. Or anything to hold it. That probably got tossed in the trash."

"By the way," Scott added. "Remember the gun we found the first day? We're pretty sure that was him. No idea what he planned to do with it, but we found a box of ammunition in a duffel bag Ross had stowed in a hidden corner of the booth. I think we were very lucky someone found that pistol before he could retrieve it."

We spent the rest of dinner dissecting the show and all that had happened, speculating about how Carrie Classics and Janice Langley would fare in the future. But we were all wiped out and headed home quickly after we finished.

Scott drove me to my apartment and asked if he could come in. I hesitated.

"I made a promise," he said. "I'd like to keep that now. You deserve to know." His voice caught on the last words. I couldn't remember hearing Scott sound nervous before.

"All right." Tired as I was, I needed to know what secret he was keeping. I had some suspicions, and I couldn't decide if I hoped they were right or not.

I offered wine or coffee, but he wanted only a glass of water. I poured one for myself as well and we sat in my living room.

His hands shook, sloshing a few drops of water onto his shirt, as we both took a few sips. Tension hung between us so thickly, I thought I could've touched it. He stared at me and his eyes closed briefly. His mouth pressed into a hard line that looked more like pain than anything else.

I wanted to touch him, to throw myself against him and beg him to make everything be all right. But he couldn't. And I didn't.

He drew a long breath and let it out slowly. "Here's the truth. I'm still a sworn officer of the Metropolitan Police Department of the District of Columbia." The words came out quickly as though he had to push them out fast while he still could. "You're sometimes too smart for your own good, Heather. I think you might have guessed."

"I suspected," I admitted. But that was the easy part to swallow. What came next wouldn't be. "What I don't know is why you're working undercover at the Market Center." And wondered if I really wanted to know. Dread settled like a sack full of bricks in my gut.

His lips pinched. "With all the shows and exhibits, you have a lot of shipments coming and going all the time there. Perfect cover for a drug distribution operation."

I choked as the water I was drinking went down the wrong way. I had no trouble believing Scott was still a cop. But someone was using the Center to distribute drugs? Maybe more than one person? I gave myself a minute to absorb it while I gasped and coughed. Scott patted my back and held the glass for me to take another drink. I shivered at his touch, but this time the liquid traced the right path from mouth to throat. He returned to his seat.

"You think Dennis might be involved in a drug thing?" I asked, once I could speak again.

"We suspected him initially, but now I'm pretty sure he doesn't know anything about it. He's been out sick most of the past year. It did give someone else a perfect opportunity, though."

That was a bit of a relief, but… "Somebody working there is involved. How many people at the Center know what you're doing there?"

"Until five minutes ago, only Janelle knew. We had to get her approval. She was horrified to hear one of her employees might be involving the Center in something so appalling."

"Janelle's known about you all along." The words sounded flat, dismayed. And not even as dismayed as I actually felt. I tried to brace myself mentally.

He nodded once, sharply.

I stared at him. Rising anger warred with a desire for his comfort. I wanted to cling to him. And I wanted to beat on his chest for lying to me for so long. Instead, I asked, "Since you're now telling me, can I assume I'm no longer a suspect?"

"I wouldn't be saying any of this if you were."

I sucked in a hard breath, struggling for control. "Thank the Lord for small favors."

He winced at my sarcasm.

"Who do you think is behind it?"

He hesitated a beat too long before answering. "I wish I knew."

"But you have some suspicions."

He didn't deny it. "Maybe. Nothing I can prove. No actual evidence at all as yet, so it wouldn't be fair for me to name names right now."

He was right, but his reticence just fueled the flames of my anger. He'd been keeping so much from me. That fury helped brace me to ask the question now burning in my gut. "Was dating me…part of the plan all along?"

He paused again. "Heather…" He reached out and took my hand, but I yanked it away. I couldn't bear his touch right now.

His mouth crooked and muscles tensed sharply, like someone reacting to a blow. "Initially, yes. But it didn't take me long to realize how ridiculous that was. You're an amazing and terrific person and completely unlikely to be doing something so sleazy. I've been attracted to you from the start. And I've wanted it to be more."

I looked down at the glass of water, blinking back the threatening tears. "I want to believe that."

His voice softened. "I wish things were different. I wish we hadn't started that way. I'm sorry for the lies and the deception. I regret that so much—more than I can tell you. I hope you'll be able to believe it and forgive me. Eventually."

He took a drink of water, draining the liquid. He stood and came to me, putting a finger under my chin to raise my face, so that our gazes could meet. His eyes were more gray than green, shadowed with pain and regret but also holding glints of determination. "I want a second chance with you. I really do, Heather. Because *I* want it. I want you. Not for any other reason. I plan to do everything I can to convince you in the future that I mean it. If you'll let me."

The silence that followed felt weighted with emotion. I couldn't say anything. Nothing would get past the huge lump in my throat.

He stood and drew me up for a quick, gentle kiss on the

forehead. "For now, though, I know you're at least as tired as I am." He turned and headed for the door. "Can I call you tomorrow?"

Since we'd worked all weekend, we'd both have the next two days off. Normally we'd spend the first day resting and do something together on the next day.

I held up both hands, palms out. "I need time."

He bowed his head. "I'll wait. But I'm not giving up. Unless you tell me it's hopeless." He left quietly.

I sat, stunned for a few minutes, in that weird space between knowing I'd been injured and feeling the full effects from it.

Then the tears came and flowed for a long time.

To be continued...

* * * * *

ACKNOWLEDGEMENTS

I HAVE MANY people to thank for help in getting this book ready. First and foremost, to my daughter and editor extraordinaire, Sarah, and my sister, Barbara, a terrific beta reader. Neither hesitates to tell me when they spot a mistake or weaknesses in the writing, and I appreciate it.

I'm also very grateful to my online critique group, the Chapter-by-Chapter Critique Group on Facebook, especially Mirella, Randy, Maria, Sharon Ann, Philip, Kayli, and Lisa, who read the entire book over the course of a year and contributed many valuable suggestions.

Thanks also to the friends and family who continue to encourage my writing efforts, especially Janet, Mike, and Ginny, my daughter, Elizabeth, and son Joe. Last but certainly not least, to my husband Jim, whose constant support and encouragement keep me sane.

ABOUT THE AUTHOR

KAREN MCCULLOUGH IS the author of almost two dozen novels in the romantic suspense, mystery, paranormal, and fantasy genres and has won numerous awards, including an Eppie Award for fantasy. She's also been a four-time Eppie finalist, and a finalist in the Prism, Dream Realm, Rising Star, Lories, Scarlett Letter, and Vixen Awards contests. Her short fiction has appeared in numerous small press publications in the fantasy, science fiction, and romance genres.

A member of Mystery Writers of America, Sisters in Crime, and the Short Mystery Fiction Society, she is also a past president of the Southeast chapter of Mystery Writers of America and served on the MWA national board.

Karen worked in trade publishing for more than ten years as an editor, managing editor, and senior web editor before leaving to start her own web design business. Now retired, she writes full time. She lives in Greensboro, North Carolina.

She invites visitors to check out her home on the web at http://www.kmccullough.com and her site for the Market Center Mysteries series, http://www.marketcentermysteries.com.

Books Available:

Mysteries
A Gift for Murder
Wired for Murder

Romantic Suspense
A Question of Fire
The Night Prowlers
Programmed for Danger
Blue December
The Detective's Dilemma
Hunter's Quest

Romance
No Time for Surprise
No Time for Regrets
No Time for Mistakes
Falling for the Deputy

Paranormal Romance/Urban Fantasy
A Vampire's Christmas Carol
Guardian of the Grimoire
The Wizard's Shield
Witch's Journey (from ImaJinn Books)
Wizard's Bridge (from ImaJinn Books)